The Intruders
In This War They Had The Advantage

Jo Dinage

Peltrovijan Publishing
P.O. Box 738
Greenbelt, MD 20768
http://www.opeart.com

The author does not guarantee and assumes no responsibility on the accuracy of any websites, links or other contacts contained in this book.

The Intruders. In This War They Had The Advantage

PRINTING HISTORY
Peltrovijan Publishing/2021

ISBN: 978-1-937143-57-2
Printed in the United States of America

The Intruders– In This War They Had The Advantage

Six Bronx teens have one thing in common–a thirst for excitement! They get that and more when they set out to explore a neglected track of land in their neighborhood and embark on an adventure of a lifetime.

After falling down a ledge, the teens find that they have traveled three centuries into the future and are stuck in the middle of a war between the two tribes that now inhabit New York City.

Now, they must pick a tribe to protect. Soon they realize that they have the advantage! They know the land–the forgotten subway lines, and where to find supplies buried in the rubble of long abandoned buildings... Unfortunately, within weeks, their adventure becomes all too real as brother turns against brother, friends become enemies and people are being killed! This is no longer fun. This is war!

Other Published Works

Mind Games

Matthew has the uncanny ability to influence people's thought. To defend himself against the bullies, Matthew is eventually forced to use his special power.

The Starlight Kids, Mystery of the Feather Burglar

With the help of her friends, Shari gets her chance to turn a boring summer vacation into a fantastic action-packed adventure.

Linked

Same age, same height, same grade—they could have been identical twins, but they were not. Yet they lived in the same imperfect world with overwhelming family problems... One was black and the other was white and they had switched!

Life After High School:
Traits that Help and Traits that Hurt

This no-nonsense text explains positive and negative traits that can help or hinder teens in their post high school life. The guide gives readers strategies, helping them to identify the path to success and to avoid the route that often leads to failure.

The Dangers of Medical Radiation

It is one of the ironies of medicine that radiation, as in x-rays, CT scans, radiation therapy and nuclear medicine can cause cancer yet can be used to detect and treat cancer. Perhaps because of this irony, most of us know very little about radiation dangers. Read how to protect yourself from medical radiation.

Chapter 1

Hamid and Derrick were sitting on Hamid's stoop trying to concentrate on another dreary game of cards when Lenny rode up.

"Hi," he said as he carefully leaned his new bike on the low fence that surrounded Hamid's home. "What say we go explore those rocks today?"

Derrick's eyes brightened. "Great idea! We'll need flashlights and stuff like that, but I could easily run home and get some."

Hamid hesitated and glanced toward his house. He wasn't supposed to leave the house. That's why he and Derrick were out here on the stoop. His parents were at work and they had left strict instructions – don't leave Lente by herself. Lente was his thirteen-year-old sister. She was inside watching TV.

"I can't leave," he reminded Derrick.

"Dog!" Derrick snapped a finger.

The other two did not comment on his bizarre phrasing. It was Derrick's trademark. He liked using odd terms instead of swearing words, and regardless of how weird, no one dared tease him at school. He was too unpredictable and was likely to punch first – regardless of the consequence. Club, Hamid's German Shepherd, was sleeping on the lower step. He was the only one to react. Club lifted one eye and gave Derrick a lazy inquiring look.

"Not you Club." Derrick absentmindedly patted the dog's head and turned to Hamid. "I forgot you told me you got to baby-sit."

Lenny wasn't giving up his idea just yet. "I could get Ginny and her friend Angela to come over."

Derrick grinned and turned to Hamid. "He just said that to let us know he and Ginny are talking to each other again."

Hamid joined in the teasing. "We ought to time how long this hot spell lasts."

Lenny scowled. "Go on, keep that up and I'll take back my offer."

Hamid held up his hands in surrender. "Okay, okay," he said as he and Derrick laughed.

"So, who is Angela?" Hamid finally stopped laughing and asked.

"Angela Yap. She's a friend of Ginny. Lives next door to her."

Hamid frowned, "Do we know her?"

"I don't think so. She doesn't come to our high school. She goes to the Catholic high. Look, I'll go get them. I just left Ginny's house and Angela was with her." Lenny was already on his bike. "I'll be back in less than half-hour."

"Hold on a second Lenny." Hamid stood up hurriedly.

"What's the problem?" Lenny asked impatiently. "If Ginny and Angela stay with Lente, she's not alone. That's what your parents wanted isn't it?"

He was right... technically. Although Hamid was sure that was not how his parents would interpret things. "Alright," he finally agreed. "We just can't stay too long. I want to get back before my parents get home.

"Sure, sure..." Derrick started packing the cards. "Hurry," he said to Lenny. "You have to go to the next block while I just live two houses down."

"I'll go in and tell Lente," Hamid was already at the front door. "We'll meet here in about half-hour, okay?"

*****

A half-hour later they were gathered outside Hamid's home.

"I still don't see why I can't come," Lente insisted.

She had been nagging since Hamid first told her his plans and he was now getting seriously annoyed. "Listen, Lente. One good reason is that *I* don't want you coming." It was years since he had used tact with his sister. He didn't want her along and he wasn't going to try to pretty up his feelings.

"She is right." Ginny suddenly joined in. "I don't see why we can't all go. Where are these rocks anyway?"

Lenny pointed up the block. "It's a sort of mountain of rocks in there."

Theirs was a block of detached single-family homes. The road ended in a lightly wooded area, which was about a four-block square. Most people avoided the woods, especially since the area was unkempt and often foul-smelling. Once, when the smell got really bad, the people in the area called the police. After a search, the police found a dead body. This only convinced everyone around that the area was to be avoided.

"You went into those woods?" Angela's eyes widened.

Hamid nodded. "Last week. We wanted to cross to the other side. Do you know there is a stream in there? Just before you get to the road, it forms a little lake."

"It's the lake that smells. I guess it's used as a dump," Derrick continued.

"Is the rocky mountain far in?" Lente asked.

"That's the funny thing." Derrick voice rose with excitement. "We followed the stream, trying to find the source. And in the middle of the woods, there is this hill, just rocks really – and the water just sort of gushes out of the rocks. So we were trying to figure out exactly where the water was coming from when we found this crack. Well... it may even be a cave. It looked like a narrow passage behind the rocks. We didn't have any flashlights so we couldn't explore it."

"The passage is hard to get to." Hamid was still trying to discourage the girls from coming. "We had to climb a good way up the rocks. It's like a mountain and the hole looked narrow and dark and there could be bats in there for all we know."

Ginny scoffed. "You won't scare me, Hamid Morgan. I still want to come."

"You make it sound like a real mountain." Lenny was equally mocking. "It was just a pile of rocks. There's no reason they can't come. The passageway wasn't even that far up the rocks."

"They aren't dressed to go cave exploring."

"Lenny says it's not a cave and what's wrong with jeans and T-shirt?" Lente asked. They were all wearing jeans and T-shirts.

"What about supplies?" Hamid asked.

"Come on, Hamid," Lenny said. "What supplies do they need? Besides, you always go overboard. I'll bet you have at least four flashlights in that backpack of yours."

"Okay, fine," Hamid was annoyed. It was true that he tended to bring more than was necessary on trips. He was the only person carrying a backpack. Lenny carried only a flashlight, and Derrick had his flashlight in a small bag belted to his waist. "Just wait. I'm going to laugh my head off when you girls start screaming."

For a minute Angela looked hesitant, however Ginny took her hand. "Don't let him scare you. It's probably not much of anything anyway."

Hamid huffed out a breath. "It's getting late. Let's go if we're going."

"What about our bikes?" Lenny was looking for a place to put his bike. He, Ginny and Angela had ridden.

"Leave your bikes behind the house," Hamid suggested.

*****

It was the middle of a hot summer day. If not at summer camp or forced to stay indoors most of the school kids hung out at the park, which had a pool, so the street was deserted as the six made their way up the block and into the woods. They followed one of the many paths that led to the lake. Even before they saw the lake, the smell greeted them. And when they finally got there, no one wanted to linger. The lake was about the size of six bathtubs placed three in a row. As they got close, they all held their noses and circled what could easily be mistaken for a garbage dump.

"Just look at this junk." Derrick kicked at a torn garbage bag.

"Don't kick it," Angela warned. "Something may come out."

"Jeez!" Lente's voice sounded muffled because she had both hands covering her nose and mouth. "I hope it doesn't smell like this the entire way."

"Here by the lake smells the worst," Lenny said. "It's

not so bad further up. Come, let's hurry."

Hamid led the way with Club immediately behind. It wasn't much of a "woods". And since the trees were not densely packed, the sun was their unrelenting company. All too soon, they were hot, sticky and irritable. Worse, beyond the lake there were no paths. They had to stay close to the stream, sometimes walking in the slushy soil along the banks. The only other option would have been to try trampling through the shrubs and bushes that covered the ground wherever a tree wasn't.

"These sneakers are ruined," Angela said. She was directly behind Club, so Hamid turned and glanced down at her sneakers. They were covered with thick black muck – the stuff that lined the stream's bank. Hamid did not need to say anything. His facial expression said it all.

Angela glared at him. "I know. We weren't really prepared for hiking. Don't even bother saying anything."

Hamid shrugged and continued walking. He wore hiking boots, so did Lenny and Derrick. All the girls wore sneakers.

After trudging along for a few more minutes they came to a bend.

"How much further?" Ginny called out.

Since Hamid didn't answer, Lenny replied. "That's the mountain of rocks we're looking at now. We just need to get closer."

Hamid looked at their mountain. As Lenny said, it really wasn't much of a mountain. First, it was all rock and not much else – no trees, not much plant life. Then it was small – maybe as tall as a two-story house. About halfway up the water just seemed to pour out of the rocks – rocks that were wet, slimy, and green with some kind of a fungus.

"Yeah, this is it." Hamid walked up to and leaned against a dry area of the rocks.

Club took the opportunity to explore the water's edge as Hamid unslung his backpack and took out a water bottle. The others watched enviously as he tipped his head back and took a few quick gulps. He didn't offer them any. This was payback time!

Derrick wiped the sweat off his brow with the back of his hand as he came up beside Hamid. "Do you think the stream water is safe to drink?"

"I don't think you should drink it," Angela cautioned. "It may be polluted."

"How can it be polluted if this is the source?" Lente asked. "And look at Club. He's drinking it. Dogs are supposed to know aren't they?"

She was right. Club had taken his full of the water and was now relieving himself at nearby tree.

"We don't know that this is the source," Hamid pointed out. "Besides, dogs don't get every sickness that we get."

"Well let's just go in and get it over with," Derrick urged. "Shirts! I'm thirsty and hungry."

"I don't see any cave," Ginny said looking up.

Lenny pointed. "It may not be a cave, but see where the rocks jut out and form sort of a shelf, right next to where the water is coming from?"

Ginny stared. Their mountain was craggy, with ledges jutting out haphazardly, forming countless natural steps. At least they wouldn't have any difficulty climbing up! The shelf Lenny spoke off was just one of a number of such rocky ledges. She nodded.

"Well if you stand on that ledge, you'll see a large vertical gap. You can't see it good from down here. You have to stand on the ledge. You'll see it then. It's this dark passageway. We think it's a cave or something."

"Time to get moving." Hamid pushed himself off the rocks. "I'll go first. Come, Club."

The climb up was easy and he was at the entrance of the passageway in a minute. Club came as far as the entrance then stopped.

"Couldn't we rest first?" Lente tipped her head up to ask. She was using a stick to get the worst of the muck off her sneakers. Ginny and Angela began copying her.

"No. We don't have enough time." Hamid called down. "We have to get back home before Mom and Dad. You can clean up your sneakers when we get back. C'mon Club. It's just a cave."

Hamid tried pulling Club by the collar, but the dog simply sat on his hunches and refused to budge. No amount of tugging got him moving.

"Leave him." Derrick had clambered up beside Hamid. "He'll stay here 'till we come out."

From below, Angela anxiously watched Club. "Maybe we shouldn't go in since Club doesn't want to go," she suggested.

"If you don't want to come, you can stay here with Club." Hamid had already picked up that Angela was more cautious and serious than her headstrong friend Ginny.

"What about the girls?" Lenny shouted as Hamid switched on his flashlight and slipped between the two rocks. "They haven't any light. Give them the extra one that you have."

Hamid's head reappeared. "I want to save my spare flashlight for any emergency."

"What emergency?" Lenny scoffed.

Hamid ignored the question. He didn't think there would be a problem; he was just extra cautious – most often unnecessarily so. "Let them walk between us and use our light."

Lenny and the girls climbed up. "Seriously Hamid, what big emergency do you think we need to prepare for?"

Club began whining as Hamid disappeared into the split between the rocks, without answering. Strangely, Club did not follow even as one by one the others followed Hamid.

The passage was long and narrow... and wet. It did not look scary, yet Lenny stopped harassing Hamid as soon as they entered. The walls were slimy to the touch. Even the floor was damp – the soil, sandy rather than muddy. Fortunately, the ceiling was high enough for them to walk upright. In a single file, they slowly followed Hamid.

Then Angela screamed.

"What is it? What's wrong?" They were all jumpy.

"Something brushed against my leg," Angela cried.

"It's only Club." Hamid bent and gave Club a huge squeeze, masking his relief. Club stood quietly, his tail thumping a beat on the ground. "So you decided to come after all, eh Club."

"C'mon let's hurry. I don't like it in here." Ginny looked around. The flashlights were casting spooky shadows on the walls.

"This place gives me the creeps" Lente agreed.

"Nobody forced you to come." However, Hamid wasn't crowing at their fears. He agreed with them. It was creepy.

"Can you see the end, Hamid?" Derrick was last in line. "We should be coming to the other side soon."

"I think we are going down, not across," Lenny muttered.

"So it's a real cave then. We are going into the earth." Ginny did not sound reassured.

"Well....There is a corner coming up. I can't see around it." Hamid had his flashlight aimed at the wall. That did not help because the weird shadows made it difficult to tell exactly what was ahead.

They squeezed around the corner then stopped dead. A huge boulder blocked the path.

"This is it. This is as far as we can go," Hamid voice reflected the relief he felt at thoughts of turning around and getting out. He used his light to scan the area.

The passage had widened slightly allowing them to stand three abreast and the combined light from the boy's flashlights illuminated the area. Not that there was much to see. A huge boulder, about ten-feet tall and four-feet wide, filled the entire height and width of the passage.

Angela gave a nervous giggle. "Doesn't it look as if someone just plugged up the passage? That boulder is an exact fit."

"Shirts! I could easily climb it." With characteristic impulsiveness, Derrick dropped his flashlight and reached up to grip the boulder with both hands. The surface was rough so he had actually found sufficient hand and foot holds to start pulling himself up when the floor started to shake and rumble. He jumped off in alarm.

"Get back...Get back! Let's get out of here!" Hamid yelled.

They all turned, but they didn't get a chance to run. The floor was disappearing from under them! There were screams and utter confusion as they felt themselves falling. The boulder vanished with a huge splash.

After what seemed like hours, but was probably only a few minutes of coughing and sneezing, Hamid slowly dragged himself up.

"Lente! Everybody okay?"

Lente! Everybody okay? His voice echoed off a distant wall.

They were okay. The flashlights, scattered around, were still casting eerie shadows. Slowly, the six scrambled to their feet, dusting off the worst of the dirt. They were all damp, courtesy of the splash the boulder had made. Club began whining and pressed his nose against Hamid's legs. As the dust settled and the noise stopped, they realized they had been fortunate. They had dropped only about four feet, onto a wide ledge. The ledge however overlooked a cavern – a huge, water-filled cavern.

"Shirts!" Derrick shivered as he looked down.

Shirts! His echo replied.

Lenny used his flashlight to search the water. There was no sign of the boulder. Yet, it had to be down there. It was a drop of almost thirty feet, which meant that the water was very deep. The cavern was about quarter the size of a football field. Looking at the now calm and still surface, they found it hard to believe the water had, only minutes before, swallowed a huge boulder.

"Do you realize that we've found the source? It's the source of the stream," Hamid whispered excitedly.

Lenny frowned. "This doesn't make any sense. How does the water get outside to the stream? It's too far down."

His echoes were the only answers.

"Can we go home now?" Lente spoke in a whisper – afraid of the strange echoes.

Hamid gave her an impatient look, then shone his

light up. "We should be able to climb out of here. It's not that far up." Just by standing upright, he was able to see into the cave passage. The cave roof now continued as the roof of the cavern. It must be enormous because his light could not penetrate the darkness, to see the other side of the cavern. The answer to Lenny's question was puzzling. How *did* the water get up?

*****

"Hello!" Ginny suddenly shouted. She giggled as she listened to her echo. After a bit even Lente lost some of her fear and began shouting for the echo effects.

Club pushed even closer to Hamid. With his tail tucked tightly between his legs he looked miserable and Hamid could not understand why. "What's wrong Club? Are you hurt?" Bending, he examined his dog, but found no sign of an injury.

"Club is like me," Lente said. "He just doesn't like caves. Can't we go now?"

Angela looked at her watch. "Do you all realize it's almost four-thirty? It's been one hour since we left home."

"Yeah. I have to wash my hair and clothes before Mom gets in or she'll have a fit." Ginny looked down at her dirty T-shirt and jeans.

They examined each other in silence as the even the walls continued rumbling with the echoes of their speech. They were all equally covered in dust and dirt. Hamid and Derrick had already removed most of the dirt from their short black hair. With their low-cut hair there wasn't much to remove anyway. Lenny, who sported a crew cut, also had no trouble. His dark blond hair was almost free of dirt. Even Lente, whose black hair was neatly braided in cornrows, had managed to get rid of most of the dirt. The same could not be said for Angela and Ginny. Angela wore her straight, waist-length black hair loose, and it was now a tangled mess.

Lenny began using his fingers like a comb to get the dirt out of Ginny's equally tangled hair. Like Angela, Ginny wore her dark brown hair loose, the curly strands reaching just below her shoulders.

"Don't worry about it," Ginny said, giving Lenny a smile. "It'll wash out."

"Let's get out of here first," Angela suggested. "Then we can think about cleaning up."

"Derrick, you go first," Hamid suggested.

Lenny objected. "Let's get the girls out first."

"No." Hamid shook his head. "Better let Derrick go. He can lead the way out."

"Oh, alright." With blatant petulance Lenny turned, looking Derrick up and down, taking in his six-feet two-inch height and said, "Need a hand up?"

Derrick gave Lenny a dirty look. Placing his flashlight on the cave floor, he casually reached and gripped the floor of the cave with both hands. He easily hauled himself up.

Ginny went next. With the help of the boys, she was able to scramble up to the cave floor. Then it was Angela's turn. Next, Hamid lifted Lente by the waist. She was the youngest and shortest, so Derrick had to reach down to pull her up. At five feet nine inches, Lenny had no difficulty climbing up by himself. That just left Club and Hamid. Club, uncharacteristically timid, was continuously whining. His tail was still tucked well down, and he refused to budge from Hamid's side.

"Come Club. You're next." Hamid grabbed at Club's collar. He planned on lifting Club, but the whines grew louder. Club did not want to leave the ledge, yet it was obvious that he was also uncomfortable where he was. The dog began backing away from Hamid. Fearful that he would back right off the edge of the ledge and into the water, Hamid stopped reaching for him. "Come *on* Club. We're trying to get out of here!"

"Come up and see if he'll follow," Lenny suggested as he watched them.

"He won't be able to climb up," Hamid said as he turned and placed his flashlight on the floor of the ledge. "Keep the lights shining down here. I'll pretend to jump up."

Club moved away from the edge as Hamid pretended to climb up. Hamid immediately released his hold on the cave floor and dropped down to the ledge. The entire ledge rumbled and shook.

"Shirts, Hamid!" Derrick cried. "Come on up! That ledge doesn't sound safe."

"I can't leave Club." Hamid slowly approached the dog, then bent and hugged him. "Come, Club. We got to go." His arms tightened around his dog. It wasn't easy lifting eight-nine pounds of whining, wiggly, dog and shoving him up to Lenny. "Grab his collar! Pull him up!"

Lenny and Lente both grabbed hold of Club's collar. With Hamid pushing and them pulling, they were able to get Club off the ledge and onto the narrow passage. Hamid then quickly scrambled up.

"Okay," Derrick urged them. "Let's get out of here now."

"What's the rush now?" Lenny had picked up on the unease in Derrick's voice.

"Remember when we were coming in how slimy and wet the walls were?" Derrick aimed his light up and down the cave wall. "Look at them now."

Using their combined lights, they stared at the walls. The walls were dry and smooth.

Hamid looked down. The floor was still sandy. It was also totally dry!

Ginny huddled closer to Lenny and Lente slipped one hand in Hamid's.

Their unease mounted as they turned the corner. "What's ahead?" Lenny called out. "Can you see any light?"

"Yeah," Derrick said. "There's a faint light ahead."

They hurried on.

"So that's it then." Derrick didn't bother hiding his relief as he squeezed past the final boulder marking the entrance to the cave. "So much for our cave exploration."

He stopped abruptly.

"Move out," Hamid called. "Don't block the entrance."

The others added their take on Derrick's action in an eerie match with their personality.

"What's wrong?" Lente asked.

"Is he hurt?" Angela tried peering past her.

"Next time, signal or something," Lenny complained. "Ginny crashed right into me."

"Just get out of the way, Derrick," Ginny yelled.

Derrick did not move. "The stream is gone!"

Chapter 2

"What do you mean the stream is gone?" Hamid anxiously tried to push forward. "Derrick! Move will you!"

The pressure of the others finally moved Derrick. Soon the six were standing on the ground, just below the rocks, looking around.

Derrick was right. There was no longer a stream. Not even a streambed. Nothing! Just woods, with the dense woods coming right up to the rocky hill!

Hamid ran his hands along the outside walls of the cave, where less than half an hour ago water flowed. The walls were dry; the soil was flaky.

Lenny gave a shaky laugh. "So, the water really couldn't make it up from that cavern."

None of the others appreciated his attempt at humor. They ignored him.

"Could we have taken a wrong turn or something?" Angela whispered.

"We couldn't have. It was a straight passage." Even so, Hamid looked up.

"I'm not going back in there," Lente said instantly, reading his mind.

"I don't believe this," Hamid muttered as he looked around.

"Can't we go back in just to check," Angela sounded desperate.

"Check for what?" Derrick was scowling. "Like he said, it was a straight passage."

"Well, we can't just stand here and do nothing." Ginny was looking around as if expecting the stream to reappear.

Hamid ran his hand along the cave wall again. "I remember reading a science fiction where some people stepped in a secret passage and stepped back in time."

Lente began crying.

"Shut up, Lente," Hamid said roughly.

"Don't shout at her," Angela frowned at him. "She's just scared."

"I want to go home," Lente wailed.

"We are all scared, and we all want to go home," Hamid pointed out. "Crying isn't going to help."

"Do you realize," Derrick inserted, "If we went back in time we're all in deep trouble?"

Now they all stared.

"What do you mean?" Lenny asked.

"Hamid and Lente are black."

"So?" Lenny still didn't get it.

"I'm black too – and Angela is Chinese...."

"I'm not full Chinese," Angela inserted. "Only my father is Chinese. My mother is Puerto Rican."

Hamid looked to the sky for inspiration. "What are you getting at?"

Derrick continued. "Ginny is Puerto Rican. So, Lenny is the only one safe. He's white."

"He isn't pure Italian," Ginny said. "He told me his grandfather was from Morocco."

"So he isn't safe either. Besides, they didn't like Italians back then."

"You're talking about slavery, right?" Hamid was now scowling.

"Oh my, God!" Ginny cried.

Hamid nodded, grimly agreeing. "If we've gone back in time, we'll all be slaves."

His comment got Lente crying harder. Hamid awkwardly patted her head.

"What are we going to do?" Ginny asked.

"I still think we should go back into the cave," Angela said.

Hamid was shaking his head. "We would have to go back onto the ledge."

"And the ledge isn't safe," Lenny was shaking his head. "No way am I going on that again."

"It was after we got off the ledge that the passage changed," Derrick said. "Remember? That's when I noticed the walls weren't wet."

Nobody had any ideas and Lente was still crying. Hamid stared at the dense woods before them. There wasn't even a path. What were they going to do? One by one, they simply sat on the rocks.

"Come, Lente," Angela said pulling the younger girl down beside her. She began hugging Lente, trying to stop her cries.

"Any ideas?" Lenny asked.

Ginny looked up at the cave. "Maybe we should try Angela's idea, and go back in."

Hamid looked at Lente who was still crying softly. "Alright," he finally agreed.

"I'll hold her hand," Angela offered.

Hamid nodded. "Okay, let's go in quickly."

It didn't take long. They were soon standing above the ledge.

"I am *not* going down there," Lenny said looking down.

Derrick shone his light around. "The walls are still dry."

"I don't think it's just the ledge," Hamid said. "Nothing feels strange anymore. Remember the creepy feelings we had when we first came in the cave? All of that is gone. And Club followed us in without whining and carrying on like he did before. I think shifting that boulder caused the whole thing."

"Well, since there's no way we can go diving in that little puddle to search for the boulder, we'd better think fast how we're going to survive."

Ginny glared at him. "For God's sake Lenny, will you shut up? Nobody likes your sense of humor."

"C'mon." Hamid had been staring blankly at the water. He now gave a dispirited sigh and turned. "Let's get out of here."

*****

Once outside, Hamid took his backpack from his shoulders. He pulled out his cell phone and flipped it open. After a minute, Angela, the only other person with a cell phone, did the same.

Angela sighed. "There's no signal."

Hamid gave a brief nod as he closed his phone. Neither phone registered a signal. "Let's find out what we have."

They emptied all pockets and bags.

Lente had brought nothing. Ginny and Angela carried small handbags. Between them they had two nail files, two combs, two makeup sets with mirrors, two pens, an IPod (Angela's), lipstick and eye makeup (Ginny's), a diary (Ginny's), change purses with $10.76 combined. Lenny also had an IPod plus a flashlight, a change of batteries, a pocketknife, a small comb and $6.24. Derrick carried two flashlights with spare batteries for both, a pocketknife, a pen and $4.54.

Hamid had a combination compass, binocular and a magnifying glass set; a pen; two pencils; a pencil sharpener; a box of colored chalk; a blank note book; a small book on cave exploration; a New York City road map; a map of New York State; coiled climbers' rope; four candles; three packs of matches; three flashlights with spare batteries for all; a pocket knife; a box of saltine crackers; two bottles of bottled water, one three-quarter full; one folded canvas sheeting; a first-aid kit with gauze bandage wrapping; and a thin plastic raincoat, rolled to a one-inch square packet.

"A rain coat?" Derrick asked. "Shirts!" His tone expressed the disbelief on the faces of the others.

"Just in case we had to pass under a waterfall or something," Hamid said defensively.

Lenny made a repulsive snort.

"Don't knock it," Ginny said. "If he wasn't so disgustingly over-organized, we wouldn't have anything. At least now we may have a halfway chance of surviving."

Her comment only served to depress them further.

"We *can't* live here," Angela's despair was palpable.

Hamid looked around. "We already tried the cave. We're.... What's that?"

From the woods, came the sounds of yapping and snarling. A dogfight? Here?

"Where's Club?" Hamid looked around frantically. "Club!" he called before rushing off in the direction of the snarling.

It was a small, rocky clearing only a few feet away and Club was in the middle of a vicious fight with a coyote.

They watched helplessly as the coyote tried to bite out a chunk of Club's neck. His collar saved him. The coyote's teeth slipped off harmlessly, and the two animals lunged at each other again.

Derrick grabbed a stout stick and ran forward. He began hammering away at the coyote's head. With vicious fury the coyote turned to confront this new attacker. Derrick backed up in surprise as the animal took aim at his neck, actually knocking him to the ground before Club attacked again – this time from behind. Club's teeth sank into the coyote's neck. The two animals were now locked together, and Club had the upper hand!

The incident had happened so fast, the others were still standing in shock. Now, as Derrick started to go after the coyote again – stick in hand – Hamid screamed at him.

"Derrick! Leave them! Are you crazy?"

Derrick ignored Hamid's shouts. He continued whacking the coyote's head until finally the animal was still. Club, who had not let go his death grip on the coyote's throat, also relaxed.

"Jeez! Is it dead?" Lente asked.

"I hope so." Derrick was breathing hard. He still clutched the stick.

"Are you hurt?" Hamid spared him a glance before rushing over to examine Club.

Derrick shook his head. The coyote's paws had landed on his chest when he was knocked over, but he had emerged from the fight without as much as a scratch.

Hamid turned his attention fully to Club. Apart from a few nicks and scratches, Club was fine. With a sigh of relief, Hamid stood and looked at Derrick. "Thanks.... Thanks for saving him, although..." he paused. How to suggest – he didn't want to upset Derrick or anything –

that it wasn't exactly sensible to attack a wild animal with a stick?

Lenny apparently didn't share Hamid's concern. "You fool! Are you stupid or something? Don't you know better than to attack a wild animal?"

Derrick's retaliation was swift and furious. "Don't call me a fool you...." He used a derogatory name for Italians.

Lenny launched himself at the taller boy. In his surprise attack, his fist connected solidly with Derrick's chin.

"Hey!" Hamid rushed between the two, pushing Derrick away with both hands.

"Lenny!" Ginny screamed as she too rushed to halt the fight. She grabbed Lenny from behind.

Hamid stood facing Derrick. Although he was an inch taller, Derrick was close to twenty pounds heavier than he was. If Derrick insisted on fighting there would be trouble. "Listen, man. Quit this. We have enough problems without the two of you fighting."

"Did you hear what he called me?" Lenny shouted, trying to twist away from Ginny.

"How many times have you both called each other names?" Hamid said, throwing Lenny a quick glance. Good! Ginny still held him. Now if only Derrick would calm down. Derrick often acted without thinking and he generally had an explosive temper that cooled in the blink of an eye. Since he wasn't now fighting, Hamid knew it would soon be safe to leave him.

"This was different," Lenny insisted.

It was. Their name calling in the past was usually gentle teasing that ended in laughter. This time it was expressed in a deliberate attempt to hurt and Derrick had never used that particular ethnic slur before.

"Let's end this," Ginny pleaded.

"Fine with me," Derrick shrugged. "If he lays off the name calling, I will too."

"Okay," Hamid turned to Lenny. "Agreed? From now on, no racial name calling."

"First, I want an apology."

"No way." Derrick was adamant. "Do you know what your problem is Lenny? You can dish it out, but you can't take it. I lost count of the number of times you used the N-word...."

"That's different and you know it," Lenny shouted.

"Well, I never liked it!"

Lenny looked to Hamid for support.

Hamid hesitated. "I don't love it.... I mean.... I know we didn't say anything..." It was fairly common at school and Lenny had only ever used the word joking, when with him and Derrick. Although he knew adults didn't like the word, somehow it had never seemed wrong to him before. It was a weird feeling. Maybe it was because they were now facing the reality of slavery.

"Let's just forget it," Ginny pleaded again. She now held Lenny's arm. "You *did* punch him back, Lenny. And we've decided not to use racial names. Let's leave it at that. We still need to figure out what to do."

Lenny gave Derrick a 'just-you-wait' look then turned and stalked off. There was silence.

Angela nervously rubbed her hands together. "What do we do now?"

"We could cook up the coyote," Derrick suggested, "For dinner."

The coyote was lying where Derrick and Club had left it. There was a small pool of blood under its head, probably caused by the neck wound Club had inflicted.

"Cook it? Yuck!" Lente said.

"Cook it how?" Ginny asked.

"In Jamaica we cooked goats whole," Derrick said. "I've watched my uncle do it. You just slit and skin it, then take out the innards. Then you put a stick through the goat and turn it over an open fire. It didn't look hard to do."

Derrick's assessment was way off. Not only was it hard, but it was also downright exhausting. They dragged the coyote back to the foot of the hill. That and getting wood for the fire were the only easy parts. At first, the idea was to skin the coyote, bring it up to the mouth of the cave, make a campfire, and cook it. Great plan! If only it had worked. After spending close to two hours just skinning the animal, they decided to leave it where it was. Tired, bloody and irritated, Derrick and Lenny forgot their quarrel and joined the squabble over how to get the stomach, the intestines and the other organs out. They ended up using their knives, rocks and sticks to pull the animal's sides apart. Three hours later, after using the sand from the cave to clean off their hands, the coyote was still cooking at the foot of the mountain.

"It's getting dark," Lente murmured.

"Well, it's past eight o'clock," Hamid muttered in return. "It's supposed to get dark." Lente lowered her eyes – her feelings apparently hurt. However, Hamid refused to feel guilty.

"I'm starving." Lenny stared at the coyote. "Who would believe a little coyote would take so long to cook."

Angela and Ginny were trying to get the worse of the tangles, and dirt, out of their hair. Angela looked up. "We can eat it with the biscuits when it's done."

Ginny scowled at the coyote. "If it ever gets done."

"Turn it again, Derrick," Hamid said. "That side looks

burnt."

Derrick was whittling sticks with his knife. He didn't look up. "It has to burn or the insides won't cook."

"Well turn it so that at least it burns evenly."

"I know what I'm doing."

Although Hamid was positive that he didn't, to maintain the peace he refrained from commenting. They were all too irritable to be reasonable at this point.

Lente came up beside him. "What are we going to do with the organs?"

"If we had a pot we could cook some soup with them," Angela suggested.

Ginny grinned. "Sure, and if we had a bed we could sleep on it."

Lente giggled. "If we could find our house, we could go home now."

"It we had... "Ginny tried again.

"Alright!" Derrick shouted. "Shut up, will you!"

"Spoil sport," Ginny muttered.

Lenny scowled. "Don't tell my girlfriend to shut-up."

Lente stopped giggling. The atmosphere immediately became charged.

Chapter 3

Derrick gave Lenny a side glance. Lenny was obviously spoiling for a fight. Derrick wasn't. He shrugged. "Okay. I won't, even if you beg me."

Lente gave a nervous giggle. There was a moment of tense silence then the others began laughing. They all knew that when she got going, Ginny could chat for hours.

Crisis averted. Hamid gave a silent sigh of relief before turning to Lenny. "Didn't the Indians use the stomach as a water bottle?"

Angela shivered realistically. "You won't find me drinking water out of that."

"They used the intestines," Lenny said. Hamid was sure he was just being disagreeable.

"No. It was the stomach," Ginny insisted.

"Well, this stomach is too small to carry water in any case," Derrick pointed out.

Lenny looked over at Club. The dog was lying, his eyes fixed on the rotating coyote. "Maybe Club will eat it."

"Club never eats raw food," Hamid's tone was absolute.

Lenny threw a piece of liver to Club. Club wolfed it down in a single gulp. Lenny grinned at Hamid, clearly pleased with himself.

Ginny smothered a laugh. "Well, I guess that solves the problem of what to do with the organs."

Hamid ignored them both. "Is the meat ready yet?" he asked Derrick.

Using the stick, one end of which he had whittled to a point, Derrick poked the meat. He then took his knife and carved off a piece of the coyote's side. "There is no blood so I guess it is cooked." He took a cautious bite. "It just tastes funny."

"Let me try a piece." Lenny stretched his hand out for some.

"It's hot," Derrick warned.

"Just give me."

Derrick handed Lenny a piece. Lenny munched thoughtfully as the others watched. "It's cooked enough for me," he declared as he licked his fingers.

Everyone agreed with Derrick. The coyote tasted funny, but it could be because they had never eaten coyote before and in any case they were just too hungry to care. Soon they were feasting on coyote meat and crackers, washed down with water from Hamid's supply.

*****

Lente didn't want to climb up the rocks again, but she was overruled. The others felt it was the safest place to sleep. They also decided to keep a fire at the cave's entrance all night, just to discourage any animals from visiting. It was really dark now and no one wanted to venture into the woods. First they stomped out their first fire and made a new one in front of the cave. Then they pulled the leftover coyote up the rock face. They also gathered twigs, sticks and small branches from the edge of the woods, saving them to replenish the fire during the night.

"You know," Hamid mused as he dumped another

bunch of twigs on the pile. "Maybe we just need to go into the cave at the exact time we did the first time to get back to our time-period."

"We didn't really check the time we originally went in," Angela pointed out.

Lente looked up from checking her 'bed' on the sandy floor of the cave. She had piled the sand to make a softer sleeping area. "We were in there at four-thirty. Remember, you told us the time."

"And we left home before three," Ginny said. She turned to Angela. "We were going to watch that show – you know – about those school kids. It comes on at three."

"Okay," Derrick said. "So tomorrow we'll go in at about three-thirty and see what happens."

"What if nothing happens?" Lenny asked.

"Don't even think about that." Angela clasped her hands over her face and bent forwards.

The others shifted uncomfortably. They weren't sure whether she was crying or praying or what. Angela was definitely a worrier. Ginny finally went over and squatted beside her. "Don't worry," she said putting an arm around Angela's shoulders. "Things will work out."

Angela nodded without lifting her head.

"Mommy is probably worried about us," Lente broke a long silence.

Hamid nodded as he pretended to be busy rearranging the twigs. He was guiltily aware that it was his fault Lente was here. If only he hadn't left home. And he shouldn't have taken Lente. His parents got in at six. It was now eight thirty. By now they would have called the police. If I get back I'll never, ever disobey them again, he promised silently.

"My Dad may think my Mom has kidnapped me,"

Derrick said.

"Why would your Mom kidnap you?" Ginny asked.

"I was living with her in Jamaica. Dad came for me last summer. I was just supposed to stay with him for the summer, but he never sent me back."

They all looked aghast, all except Hamid. He already knew Derrick's story.

Angela looked up; her eyes were suspiciously red. "That's awful. Don't you miss her?"

Derrick shrugged. "Sort of." He looked away for a second, then shrugged again. "I like it here. Besides, she was always mad about Dad leaving me in the first place... always mad about something. I was getting tired of dealing with that."

Ginny was still shaking her head in disbelief. "Have you seen her since... or spoken to her or anything?"

Derrick grimaced. "Yeah. She calls often. It always ends with her crying and me getting fed-up."

"Why can't she come and take you?" Angela asked.

"What about the police?" Lenny said. "If she knows where you are why don't they take you back?"

"She can't come, 'cause she needs a visa to visit America and she doesn't have one. And she didn't tell the police. I don't think she really wants me back. She's just mad with Dad for taking me like that."

As he absently patted Club's head, Hamid noted their shocked expressions. Sure, they were shocked, especially since they couldn't even begin to understand Derrick's casual attitude. They all came from two-parent homes, even Ginny who lived with her mother and stepfather. He sort of understood, because he had been friends with Derrick for almost a year now. Not only had he heard it all before, more than once he had put up with Derrick's sullen fury only because he knew his friend was hurting. Derrick may act cool and casual now, yet Hamid knew he bitterly resented his father for ignoring him while he was growing up. He also had problems relating to his mother because his mother did not really want him back.

"I sometimes wish my Ma would leave Dad." Lenny said, and then added morosely. "And I used to wish I could leave... who would believe I'd get my wish granted."

"What's wrong with your dad?" Derrick asked.

"He drinks."

The emotionless response had Ginny patting his arm. "He gets stinking drunk one night every week," she explained.

"Only one day?" Angela was confused.

"Once a week is bad enough. Even Ma stays clear of him when he comes in on a Friday night. Sometimes Monday comes along and he's just sobering up."

This was news to Hamid. "Has he always been like that?"

Lenny snorted. "Always. Whenever he hits Ma or one of us he acts like he's sorry and for a week he may stay sober. It never last. And I lost track of the number of times he says he's going for treatment."

"Well," Derrick commented. "He must have some control if he only gets drunk on Fridays."

"It's the fear of losing his job that keeps him sober," Lenny said with a grunt.

Ginny put her arms around him in comfort. "Don't think about him. You can't change him." She added teasingly, "Think about your brother stealing your baseball cards when you don't show up tonight. That ought to cheer you."

"I'll kick his butt if he does."

"He'll probably beat you," Ginny turned to the others. "Johnny, his brother, is just as tall as Lenny. And Johnny is only fourteen."

"Not only will your sisters take your things they'll take over your room," Lenny retaliated.

Ginny scowled.

Hamid grinned. "How many sisters do you have? Every time I turn around somebody tells me so-and-so is your sister."

"Five." Ginny's voice dripped resentment. "And they are only half-sisters. My step-dad is still trying for his precious boy prince."

"I always wish I had even one sister," Angela said.

"Believe me," Ginny said fervently. "You're not missing anything."

"Is there only you?" Lente asked.

Angela nodded. "My mother can't have any more children. I heard her and my dad discussing it one night. They think I don't know, so when I want to upset them, I start begging for a baby brother or sister." She grinned suddenly. "It so upsets my mother."

"I do that sometimes too," Ginny said. "I listen to them at night. That's how I find out stuff. That's why I know they all hate me."

"Ginny!" Angela was shocked.

Lenny was nodding. "It's true. You should see how they treat her. Everything goes to the other girls. She gets the leftovers."

"Even your *mother* hates you?" Lente asked.

Ginny was staring at the fire. "Maybe she don't exactly hate me. But..." She paused, and hunched over, pitching her voice lower to hide her emotions. "I still think that deep down, she will be glad if I never show up again. With me around she keeps having to choose between me and my step-dad." She gave a wry smile as she looked up. "You know, when I think about it, I don't know how she puts up with me. I know I cause a lot trouble." She took a deep breath. "I can't help it. It just sort of comes out sometimes. And sometimes I just get mad and do things deliberately."

Lenny gave her arm a quick squeeze. "Forget about them."

The others nodded in agreement and for the next few minutes reminisced on their parents and friends until one by one they fell asleep, except for Hamid and Angela. Since they had first watch, they were soon the only ones talking. Club was most likely a great watch dog, but they had agreed that someone should keep watch at all times – two and a half hours each. Hamid got paired with Angela because he wanted first watch and Lente was too sleepy to stay up. So Lenny and Ginny took second watch and Lente was paired with Derrick for third.

*****

The next morning, after a breakfast of leftover coyote and crackers, they sat by the base of the hill. The girls sat on rocks and tried cleaning their sneakers and fixing up in general.

"I wonder when I'll get a change of clothes." Ginny brushed her hair as she scowled at her dirty T-shirt and jeans.

"I feel sticky and horrid." Lente was braiding Angela's hair. She did one thick braid down Angela's back to keep it neater.

"I know what you mean." Angela grimaced as she pulled on her sneakers. She hadn't been able to get much of the dirt off.

Derrick stood up. "Let's explore. After all, we have until three-thirty," he said. "Maybe I can find a souvenir."

"No," Hamid objected sharply. "Don't take anything. The whole plan may not work if we take something we didn't come with."

"What about the coyote?" Angela asked. "We ate it."

"That's on its way out," Lenny grinned.

Ginny jabbed him in the ribs. "Don't be disgusting."

However, Hamid was frowning.

"Do you really think that will matter?" Angela asked worriedly.

"I don't know." Hamid rubbed the side of his head. It was way too early to sort out problems like these. "Maybe just by eating it we've changed things."

"That can't count," Derrick objected. "If that was so, we would never get back. Every twig we touched – everything would make a difference."

"Then we'll never get back," Lente wailed.

Hamid gave her a harassed look. "Don't be silly." He turned to the others. "Okay, let's explore." He was willing to try anything to take his mind off this particular problem.

*****

The woods were thick, dense and unyielding. They were also dark and cool, although it was a sunny summer morning.

"It's not that dark. We don't need to use the flashlight," Hamid said as Derrick turned on his light. "Besides, we need to conserve the batteries," he cautioned.

For once Derrick obeyed. Instantly and without question, he switched off his light.

The Intruders. In This War They Had The Advantage

First, they tried clearing a path in the general direction of the stream, as they knew it. That didn't work. It was early July; everything that could grow had grown. After a few feet the way was blocked by a fallen tree. Derrick tried climbing over the tree.

"I can't jump down from here," he called to the other five. "There are too many branches and things. And it may not hold me up. I can't even see the ground."

"Come down," Hamid urged. "The last thing we need is for you to break a leg."

"Let's turn back." Lente looked worried. "It is too easy to get lost."

"I have the compass," Hamid pointed out impatiently. "You don't get lost with a compass unless you are dumb or something. We are heading northwest."

"Let's just go around the tree," Lenny said.

"We need something, maybe... sticks or something... to help us clear a path." Derrick waved in the direction of the thick woods as he jumped off the tree trunk.

They broke branches from trees, and then continued. The branches weren't ideal, but they did make clearing the way that much easier.

"Aren't you afraid Club will wander off?" Angela asked as she watched Club. The dog seemed to be doing his own exploration, bounding off into the woods every now and again only to return to Hamid's side, panting.

"Lost?" Hamid looked incredulous. "Club? Never! We go walking a lot and I don't ever have to keep him on a leash. He never wanders far from me. And he'll come back immediately if I call him."

"I'm getting hungry," Ginny called after a while. "What are we going to do for lunch?"

They had finished the last of the coyote and Hamid's

crackers for breakfast.

Lenny looked at Club. "Maybe we could train Club to find us food."

"What a dumb idea," Derrick sniffed.

Lenny stiffened. Before he could say anything, Hamid glared at Derrick. "Cut it out."

Derrick grinned. "Yes Pa."

"One of these days you'll get that grin knocked off your face," Lenny muttered.

"Thank God it won't be by you," was Derrick's immediate response.

"Listen, I've had it with you two." Hamid scowled at each of them. "When we get back, you can kill each other for all I care, but right now I'm not going anywhere with you both acting like a two-year-old."

"You should just leave them," Ginny said. "I think they get a kick out of annoying each other. Let's look out for food."

Angela grinned at her. "Don't tell me you expect to find food lying on the ground?"

After another quick look at Lenny and Derrick, Hamid decided to take Ginny's advice. He turned to Angela. "We can't eat anything dead if we don't know what killed it."

Angela rolled her eyes, "I know that!"

"C'mon," Derrick urged them. "Let's just go."

Tentatively, Lente slipped her hand into Hamid's. "What if we meet somebody?"

He glanced down at her hand in surprise – Lente was usually too busy distancing herself from him and asserting her independence to want his comfort. However, he did not comment on the hand holding. "We'll just stay together. Club will warn us if anyone comes near."

They continued. Twice they had to take detours,

because even with the sticks it was hard going. Then they came to another clearing. This area was not entirely free of woods, but there were less trees and shrubs. In fact.... Derrick looked closely at the ground.

"Hey look! This was a road."

A road! What's a road doing in the woods? The thought was in everyone's mind.

"Look." Derrick pointed to definite areas of asphalt.

"That's not possible." Like the others, Lenny was examining the ground. "They didn't have roads in the past. Not like this."

Lente tugged at Hamid's hand to get his attention. "Wait a second Lente." Hamid bent to check out Derrick's road theory.

"This is important," Lente insisted. "I have to tell you now... now that the others are busy."

Hamid got up and gave her a distracted glance. "Tell me what?"

"Ginny and Lenny were kissing and things last night," she whispered.

Hamid looked around in embarrassment, but both Ginny and Lenny were busy examining the area with Derrick and Angela.

"Lente!"

"I got up early and saw them."

"That's their business."

"What if Ginny gets pregnant?"

Hamid's mouth dropped open. He quickly closed it. "Listen, Lente," he began, feeling pressured. "I'm not their parent. What do you want me to do? I can't stop them. Besides, you don't get pregnant by kissing!"

"I know that!" She glared at him in outrage. "They may do it! You have to talk to Lenny."

Hamid could just imagine himself talking to Lenny and getting a punch for his efforts. The other kids at school usually knew to keep out of his way. Lenny in a bad mood would pick a fight with a saint. Besides, he was sure they had already, 'done it.' Then again, as far as he was concerned, there was nothing wrong with kissing. He had felt like kissing Angela last night.... Just to shut Lente up, he agreed. "Alright, I'll see."

"Hey! Look!" Derrick called. "Houses!"

Hamid and Lente hurried over to join the others. Sure enough, there were houses – dilapidated, rundown houses that looked as if they had been left untended for years. Some even looked as if a fire had swept through them. After wandering around, they realized that the entire area was lined with houses. Forgetting caution, they hurriedly approached one of the houses.

"Lenny," Ginny cried. "This looks like our block. Look! That would be Mrs. DeMartini's house."

"I don't know," Lenny said as he looked around. The houses were eerily similar, yet there were differences that could not be explained by age and neglect alone. The last time they saw it, Mrs. DeMartini's house had a bright green awning. Nowhere in the rubble was there any evidence of awnings, green or otherwise. "It looks different."

Hamid began to laugh. "We didn't go back in time. We went forward."

Chapter 4

Lenny slowly approached one of the houses. It looked as if a bomb had landed smack bang in the center of the house. The roof had long since caved in, taking most of the outer brick walls with it. As an added insult, three trees – almost fully grown – were competing for light and space where once a front porch stood.

"What could have happened?"

Hamid shook his head. "Whatever happened must have happened ages ago. It takes more than fifty years for trees to grow that big."

"Let's go in." Derrick walked up what was once a driveway. "Look! This one looks burnt out."

"No!" Lente grabbed Derrick's arm. "Suppose there are dead people in there."

Derrick gave the houses an assessing look. "I don't think so. These houses look as if they have been abandoned for years and years. Even if someone died in there, they would be nothing but skeletons by now."

Angela shivered. "That's even worse. Suppose we find my parents in one of the houses."

Hamid looked at his watch. "There is no time anyway. If we hope to get into the cave at three-thirty, we have to get going. It took almost three hours to get here. Come Club!"

As Club bounded toward him, Hamid checked his cell

phone again.

"Anything?" Lenny asked.

"Nothing." Hamid slipped the phone into his bag. "What about you Angela?"

"Nothing and my phone is just about dead anyway. I didn't charge it before we left."

They turned away. Derrick however, stood irresolutely.

"Come *on*, Derrick!" Hamid called. "We have to get back."

Derrick reluctantly came. "It seems such a waste not to find out what happened. Suppose it's something we could prevent?"

"We can't change the future," Lenny pointed out,

"Well," Ginny said, "before yesterday, I didn't think we could just vanish from the present into the future."

Angela sighed. "I don't know what to believe anymore. I just want to get home. My parents are worrying themselves sick right now."

"Mine too," Lente murmured.

They walked in silence trying to stick to the path they had previously cleared. Lenny abruptly spoke out, "We didn't have lunch."

"Tell me something I don't know," Derrick muttered.

Lenny ignored him. He pointed. "That looks like a plum tree. What say we stop and get some?"

"Where?" They followed his pointing finger.

Hamid nodded. "Okay. Let's take enough to last a while."

Getting to the tree proved some doing, but they made it. Using sticks, they first tried knocking down the plums, then Derrick and Lenny climbed the tree and threw down as many plums as they could get. It wasn't an efficient system. Half the plums were disappearing into the undergrowth. Never mind. They had fun finding them, so no one suggested changing the process. Even Club joined the act, barking wildly and scrambling into the bushes for plums. Finally, with Hamid's raincoat filled, they decided to call it quits – it was almost three. They ended up carrying the raincoat like a hammock and spent the rest of the journey walking and eating.

Their high spirits lasted all the way to the foot of the rock mountain. Then one by one they sobered up. This was it. If their plan failed....

"Do we take the plums or no?" Angela asked.

"Leave them. Just give me my raincoat."

The rest of the plums were dumped at the cave's entrance. Hamid folded his raincoat, and they started the walk into the cave.

"The walls are dry," Lenny was shining with his light, up and down.

No one commented. All too soon, they were standing above the ledge.

Lenny looked down. "It will never take our weight."

"It did before," Derrick said. "How about I go down and we see what happens."

"I don't think..." Hamid began.

"We could use your rope." Derrick's eyes were glinting with suppressed excitement.

Hamid realized something. For Derrick this was still one huge adventure. Derrick expected to get back home. It was just a matter of when. He, on the other hand, wasn't so sure. He looked around at the expressions of the others. They were all hopeful, except for Lenny. Lenny wore his, 'well it might just work but I wouldn't count on it,' expression. Hamid met his gaze. Lenny shrugged. With a shrug of his own, Hamid lowered his backpack and bent to take out the rope. Club pressed a cold wet nose to his face. Hamid patted him absentmindedly.

"Okay," he said to Derrick. "We'll tie this around your waist, and we'll lower you down."

"We need to anchor the rope somewhere," Lenny warned. "If the ledge gives way, we don't want Derrick dragging us all in the water."

Derrick gave the rope around his chest an experimental tug as Hamid looked around. There was nowhere to anchor the rope.

"Let's all lie down," Hamid suggested, "We each hold the rope. Lenny, you could hold this end and lock your ankles around the corner."

"That's not going to work," Lenny objected. "I would have to carry everybody's weight or Derrick will pull us all over."

Derrick turned on him. "You are going to object to everything aren't you? What's the big deal?" He was clearly exasperated. "The ledge isn't going anywhere. I'm going down."

Suiting action to words, he started climbing down.

"Wait!" Hamid cautioned him.

"I hope you can swim," Lenny threatened, as Derrick gripped the edge of the cave floor. "'Cause if you go down now I'm gonna let go my end."

Derrick stopped. "What is it with you all? Do you love this place?" He glared at them. "I want out of here. If we stand here much longer, it's going to be past the time." He stood up, pulled the rope off his head and threw it down. Then, before anyone could stop him, he jumped to the ledge below.

"Oh my God!" Ginny screamed.

The ledge rumbled and shook. Hamid was furious. He ran forward while screaming at the others. "Back up! Everyone back up!" As the girls and Lenny backed away from the edge, Hamid threw one end of the rope to Lenny. "Go around the corner then get everyone to hold this end."

Hamid checked Lenny's position. A loud splash brought his attention back to Derrick. The ledge was disintegrating! Whole chunks were falling in the water below. Hamid quickly tossed the other end of the rope to Derrick.

"Put it on! Tie it around your chest!" he yelled.

Derrick quickly complied. He had dropped to the ledge in a crouch. With the rope safely around his chest he slowly stood up. Hamid checked Lenny's position again. Lenny and the girls had backed out to the main passage. Satisfied that they were safe, he got on his belly and wiggled to the very edge.

Derrick took a cautious step forward. There was a horrifying cracking sound.

"Is he okay?" Lenny called.

"Yeah. He's coming," Hamid called back. "Hurry, Derrick. There's a crack forming right at your left foot."

Derrick looked down. It was a huge crack, running zigzag from the edge of the ledge inwards. He took the next few steps quickly, and then grabbed hold of the cave floor. One quick heave and he was up.

Hamid stared at the ledge. Although the crack had widened, the ledge held. "He's up," he called to Lenny and the others.

Lenny reappeared. "You..." He swore viscously! "We should have left you down there."

Ginny griped his arm, but Lenny impatiently brushed her off.

"Leave it Lenny," Hamid advised after a quick glance at Derrick. He knew Lenny wanted to continue ripping up Derrick however, he didn't see it making any sense berating Derrick publicly. Later they would talk. They weren't in the Bronx they knew anymore. Derrick had to understand that his impulsive behavior could easily get him or all of them killed.

Naturally, Lenny did not shut up. "Leave it! Leave it! That was the most stupid, the dumbest.... Only an idiot...."

"I didn't beg you to rescue me," Derrick said tightly. He dragged off the rope, threw it down, then brushed past the others, heading for the cave's entrance.

Hamid glared at Lenny. "You couldn't keep your mouth shut could you?"

"Were you going to let him get away without saying anything?" Lenny challenged him.

"He already knew what he did was dumb," Hamid pointed out. "Saying it out loud didn't help any. Besides, I would have said something to him privately where it wouldn't make him feel...." He stopped as he saw Lente about to slip away. "Where're you going?"

Lente did not stop. "I just want to see where Derrick went."

Hamid turned back to Lenny.

"Tact. That's what he lacks," Ginny said before Hamid could speak again. "I've told him a thousand times he has no tact."

Hamid acknowledged Ginny's comment with a nod and gave Lenny a final glare before bending to pick up his rope. Despite Ginny's tough talk she was a natural peacemaker. He would have to remember that the next time he needed a mediator to keep things calm.

The others watched and waited in silence as he rolled

the rope and repacked it. When Hamid was finished, with the silence still unbroken, they made their way to the outside.

*****

Derrick and Lente had already climbed down. Both were sitting on the rocks talking quietly. As soon as they saw the others approaching, they stopped.

As Derrick turned away Lente looked up challengingly.

Hamid ignored her look. Lente was too soft. Back home she was always championing the underdog and trying to get their parents involved in random aid projects. She was probably feeling sorry for Derrick. "At least we know now that it's the boulder and not the ledge that shifted us into another time."

Everybody started talking at once, as if determined not to allow another minute of silence. Equally abruptly, the talking stopped, and the uncomfortable silence resumed.

Angela cleared her throat. "I think I know why we don't have a stream anymore."

"What has that got to do with anything?"

"So what?"

"I bet...."

"Why?"

The confused jumble of conversation again came to an abrupt halt, stopping just as suddenly as it had begun. Again there was a silence.

Angela gave a forced laugh before trying again. "I think that maybe years ago the water table was higher, and water was able to seep down the rocks and form the stream. As the water level dropped the stream dried up."

"You're probably right." Hamid said absently. His mind really wasn't on the question. He was looking at Derrick, wondering what to do next.

"Yeah," Ginny grumbled. "And that helped us a lot."

"Well," Lenny said with a mockingly bright smile. "At least it tells us we are stuck here for good."

"Lenny!" Ginny cried.

Lenny turned to her, visibly angry. "Listen. We may as well face facts. We are never getting back."

Angela looked at Hamid. "You think it's hopeless too, don't you."

He did. Deep down, he did…. He just wasn't ready to admit that out loud. Not yet. Besides, he could not crush Angela's hopes. Instead, he looked around. "I don't know… I don't know. Look, let's just concentrate on living. It's only four. We need to get dinner going. Like more fruits… or something."

Lente started crying again. Derrick awkwardly patted her back as he glared at Hamid. He obviously expected Hamid to reassure her.

In exasperation, Hamid ran a hand across the back of his neck and paced in a small circle. He felt totally helpless. "I don't know… I don't know. What do you want me to say? I hope we'll be able to get back. I just don't know…."

There was a tense silence. Angela went to sit on the other side of Lente.

"It'll be okay Lente. It'll be okay," she comforted the younger girl.

"We could go back to the houses," Lenny suggested. "Maybe we can pick up something useful."

Ginny forced a grin. "Yeah. Like pots or something."

Hamid immediately shook his head. "No. Maybe

tomorrow. It's too late now. It took close to five hours just to get there and back. The last thing we need is to get stuck in these woods after dark. Let's just look around this area. There must be more fruit trees close by."

They started to move off. Derrick stood up abruptly. "Wait a minute," he said. As they all stopped and stared at him, he continued. "Look." He paused, looked down and kicked at a pebble then looked up again. "I'm sorry about back there in the cave."

Hamid felt a wave of relief; he had been wondering how to approach Derrick. He now gave Derrick a broad grin. "Help us find dinner and it will be forgotten."

"Just don't do it again," Lenny warned, his gaze deliberately challenging.

Derrick started to say something then turned away, showing uncharacteristic restraint.

Hamid gave Lenny an irritated look. "Come. Let's stick together."

They found an apple and another pear tree, and made three trips from the trees and back to the cave's entrance carrying the raincoat loaded with fruits. It was dark by the time they had their fill of fruits, so they made another fire and settled down for the night. By common consent they kept the same partners as the night before. However, this time around Lenny and Ginny took first watch followed by Derrick and Lente.

*****

They were all up early the next morning.

"We need water to drink and to wash with," Angela said as she combed out her hair.

"Yeah," Derrick said as he slapped his jeans, trying to remove the loose sand. "I'm beginning to smell myself."

Lenny looked up from where he was stomping out the fire. "We can already smell you."

"Get lost," Derrick said lazily.

"I'm already lost," Lenny retorted.

Hearing them, Hamid exchanged a grin with Ginny. Things were back to normal. Lenny and Derrick had resumed their casual teasing.

"If we can get an old pot or something, we could lower it down into the cavern and collect water." Angela was still fixated on getting water.

Hamid nodded. He was perched on a low ledge munching on an apple. "Good idea. We'll go to those houses and collect whatever we can."

"And find out what happened," Derrick said.

"Maybe," Hamid had no intention of agreeing to the impossible.

"Wouldn't it be great if we found out what happened then went back and warned everyone," Derrick was warming up to idea of himself as a hero. "We'd be famous."

"We'd be in the news and everything," Lente agreed.

Hamid snorted. "Let's keep this real."

"It could happen," Derrick insisted.

Lenny started to say something, but with rare tact, and a brief glance at Lente, changed his mind.

Hamid jumped to the ground. "Yeah, right. I got to go," he said, starting toward the woods.

Lenny hurried after him.

"What do you think happened?" Lenny asked as soon as they had walked away.

"If I knew that, I would probably know how to get us back to our time period."

"Do you really think we'll get back?"

"Don't start, Lenny."

"I kept my mouth shut back there didn't I?"

"It must be the pears."

Lenny gave him a friendly push.

They found a private spot to use the bathroom before returning to the camp.

*****

After finishing their breakfast of fruits, they started out. The journey was much easier now that they had trampled the path twice before, so it was shortly after nine that they reached the houses.

"We have to be careful," Hamid warned. "These houses look likely to fall down any minute."

"How will we get in to search for stuff?" Angela worried.

"If this is Ginny's block the next one should be ours. I'm just going to cut through here and check it out." Derrick suited action to words and started walking towards what looked like a former driveway.

"Hold on! Derrick!" Hamid shouted. Derrick was genuinely puzzled as he looked around. Hamid gave him an exasperated look. "We should keep together. Either we all go together, or we don't go at all."

"Hamid," Derrick spoke slowly, as if to a small child. "Look around you. This place is totally deserted. No one has been here for centuries if not longer."

Hamid hesitated. He still believed they should stick together, but a quick glance convinced him that there was no way he would be able to get Derrick to agree. If he forced the issue, he would lose what little authority he had. No one had elected him leader. It was just natural for him to assume that position. The difficulty was his leadership style. He led by consensus. Sure, he could try dictating, but was not a comfortable fit for him, besides there was no guarantee that they would follow. He now shrugged his shoulders.

"Okay, go ahead. I still think you should wait, so be careful. If you meet anyone don't shout. Just get back here as fast as you can."

"Sure... sure..." Derrick said with a half laugh as he disappeared into the denser undergrowth that used to be a back yard.

Hamid felt he was being patted on the head – like a dog. He remained silent, still uneasy as he watched Derrick leave.

"What do we do now?" Lente asked.

"Check these houses for stuff," Lenny said. "Come on."

For about an hour, they collected supplies by carefully climbing into the ruined houses. Derrick was right. These houses had been deserted for centuries. There were no skeletons – no sign of life. Ginny, Lenny and Angela found their homes, but all admitted that the houses were somehow different, and it was unlikely that their parents had lived there just before the houses were abandoned.

"Maybe they moved," Angela said. "I know my parents. When I didn't show up they probably didn't want to live in the house."

The others silently agreed. Hamid didn't even want to think about his parents. What had they done when they believed both he and Lente were dead? It was just too horrid.

They continued their collection. The items varied: Two iron pots that looked leak free; some rusty looking spoons, knives and forks; three fairly decent mugs; scraps of metal that they decided to use as plates if necessary.

"Hey!" Lenny shouted. "Look what I found!"

Derrick was nowhere to be seen, but the others gathered around. It was a vegetable garden, overgrown with weeds and other plants…. Although….

"Is that broccoli?" Lente asked doubtfully.

Lenny pulled up the plant. "Food!" He cried gleefully.

In addition to the broccoli, there were potatoes, asparagus and a few other root vegetables. They took as much as they could carry – and were about to move to the next house – when Derrick came rushing back.

"Hamid! Hamid! Come quick!"

"Keep your voice down!" Hamid hissed. He glanced around to check on Club who was digging for some mysterious treasure nearby. "What's up?"

"There is someone in one of the houses!"

Chapter 5

"Oh my God!" Ginny cried.

"A live person?" Lente asked in a whisper.

Derrick nodded. "He's caught under a roof beam. He's just lying there. When I went in, I was making a lot of noise and his eyes sort of opened a little. And he sort of moaned."

"You mean he's stuck?" Hamid looked worriedly in the direction Derrick pointed.

Derrick nodded, "Looks like."

"We can't leave him in there," Although Hamid said the words aloud, he did not move. Instead, he looked at the others.

Lenny nodded, "We have to check. Let's go and see."

As they approached the house, Club began barking. Hamid shushed him quickly and they cautiously made their way closer. The boy was about their age or maybe a few years older and he was lying in the rubble of what may once have been the basement. The living room had collapsed inward, and a huge beam of wood was lying across his lower left leg.

"You saw him move?" Ginny asked doubtfully. Hamid shared her doubt. The boy looked dead.

"Well... not move exactly. He sort of opened his eyes and he made a sound."

The boy did neither while they watched. His wore what looked like a sleeveless T-shirt garment and a multilayered bloomer – clothing wrapped around his hips and upper legs. He also had weapons. A crudely made bow and a pouch containing arrows were at his side. Hamid looked closer. The boy had curly, black hair, and although he looked unnaturally pale, under normal circumstances his natural complexion was likely similar to a deep tan.

Finally, Hamid climbed in further and, with an eye on the exposed sky, cautiously lowered himself into the rubble. Up close the boy smelt horrible. Hamid placed his hand nervously on the boy's chest. He could feel a heartbeat! The boy's eyes flickered and opened. Hamid found himself looking into pain-filled dark pools. As he drew back in alarm, the eyes pleaded with him to stay.

The boy was obviously trying to talk. His mouth opened and closed, but no sound emerged.

Hamid nodded, once, and then experienced a jolt of sheer panic as the boy's eyes closed again. His hand shot forward involuntarily and rested on the boy's chest again. The heartbeat was still there. Good! Although the eyes did not open again, his panic subsided. The boy was not dead.

"Is he still alive?" Angela called.

"Yes…. I think." Hamid gestured to the heavy beam. "We have to get this off his leg." After taking a closer look, he turned to Lenny. "Think we should move it?"

Lenny carefully climbed in. "I don't see why not. It's not supporting anything now…. Hey! Derrick!"

"Coming." Derrick scrambled into the basement. He and Lenny took opposite ends of the beam while Hamid stayed in the middle. Within minutes they had freed the boy's leg.

Hamid gave the exposed leg a dubious look. It looked awful. It was blue-black and swollen, but at least there were no exposed bones. "First let's get him out of here then

Angela can take a look at his leg."

"Angela?" Lenny asked.

Hamid nodded. While keeping watch last night Angela had mentioned that she wanted to be a pediatrician. Back home she tried to read all she could about medicine and doctors.

"She knows a bit about medicine," he now explained.

"Should we come down?" Ginny called.

"No," Hamid said. "There's no space. It's better if we bring him up."

Getting the boy out wasn't easy. They eased him onto one of the rotting pieces of wood, but that didn't work. When they tried to move him, he woke up fully and began moaning in pain. His moans turned to a scream of pure agony as the wood snapped and he slipped from their grasp.

"Oh no! You killed him," Lente screamed.

The wood had snapped in the center, so Hamid and Lenny were still supporting the boy's lower legs, while Derrick had an arm under each of the boy's shoulders. The boy's bottom however had slipped almost to the ground causing his body to fold into the letter V.

Hamid looked at the now unconscious boy. Well, at least he isn't feeling anything now.

"Let's move him quickly before he wakes up."

"Tie the broken leg to the wood first," Angela called.

"With what?" Lenny asked. "You know Hamid will never agree to cut his precious rope into strips."

Scowling, Hamid removed his belt, "With this," he said as he shook the belt in front of Lenny's face.

Lenny did not back down. "Notice he didn't suggest his rope," he said to the group at large.

"Just tie his leg and shut up," Hamid retorted.

"I don't believe this," Derrick cried gleefully. "This one is for the record books. *Our Hamid* has lost his cool. *Our Hamid* is actually shouting."

"Derrick!" Hamid said dangerously.

Derrick and Lenny dissolved into laughter. They were still chuckling, despite Hamid's fuming looks, as they focused removing their belts, supporting the boy's legs and getting him out. Fortunately, the boy remained unconscious throughout the ordeal. And fortunately, Hamid punched neither of them, although he was tempted.

Once outside the house, they all sat around while Angela examined the leg.

"Well, he was lucky," she said. She stood and dusted her hands together. "His leg is not broken, it's just bruised."

"That's not broken?" Ginny was accurately expressing their collective doubt.

"Well, I don't know for sure. I mean…. I'm not a doctor or anything."

Hamid got up impatiently. "You said it's not broken. Is it or isn't it? Make up your mind."

"Well…. I'm not sure…."Angela began.

"Oh, shut up!" he said rudely.

Angela lapsed into hurt silence. Ginny glared at him. Even Lente and Derrick were giving him dark looks.

Lenny just looked amused. "I say it's halfway broken," he said. "You know…. Hey!" He stopped as Hamid stalked off.

Feeling thoroughly fed up and disturbed, Hamid walked over to the trees and began checking tree limbs. He liked order and for him uncontrolled situations were unnerving. He ignored Lenny, who had followed him, and broke two stout branches from the nearest tree. After a minute of watching as Hamid began stripping the branch with his knife, Lenny picked up the other limb and did likewise.

"You need to relax and stop taking things so seriously," Lenny advised as he added the final touch to the now smooth stick,

Hamid gave him a derisive look.

"Well, you needn't go as far as I do," Lenny grinned, fully understanding Hamid's mockery.

Hamid didn't bother answering and Lenny continued working beside him in silence. Hamid was glad for the silence since he didn't feel much like talking. Lenny was most likely right. But he just didn't see himself changing his personality.

Lente always said he was boring, and he was in complete agreement. There was no reason that he could think of why Lenny and Derrick stuck with him. He certainly had no other friends, and they were an unlikely trio at school. They all had such different personalities.

He liked order, he liked being prepared and organized and he did not like surprises. He had never once gotten into trouble at school. Lenny and Derrick had both been suspended numerous times for fighting. Lenny's mouth often got him in trouble and other kids avoided Derrick because they didn't know what would trigger him. He started fights regardless of his chances of winning, often times with someone twice his size, just because the person looked at him wrong.

Hamid had aborted countless fights by dragging Derrick away before things got too crazy. That was also how he and Lenny become friends. He had helped Lenny when two other boys had cornered Lenny with plans to beat him senseless. Hamid had intervened and saved

Lenny's skin. The other kids at school now knew to leave the three of them alone, since attacking one meant taking on all three.

Finding this boy here was a complication that they did not need. For a few minutes he worked at the limb furiously until he felt a measure of calm, then slowly he eased his pace.

The others trickled over.

"What are you making?" Lente asked.

"We have to carry him back to the cave." Lenny had guessed Hamid's intent.

"What if…." Ginny's voice trailed off.

Hamid looked at her. "We can't leave him here."

Nobody disagreed with his unequivocal response, they just were not happy. Like Hamid, they all recognized that for better or worse, this represented a massive change. They made a makeshift stretcher by knotting the four ends of Hamid's canvas sheeting to the two sticks. The boy was still unconscious when they lifted him on it.

"We should give him some water…. Well maybe some of the juices from the fruits." Angela murmured. "I think he may be dehydrated. He must have been lying in that basement for some time."

"Well since we don't have water, he'll have to get fruit juice," Ginny said.

Lenny took up a plum. "Anyone with an electric juicer?" he asked, with a mock serious expression.

"Give me." Ginny grabbed the plum out of his hand and turned to Hamid. "Let me have one of those gauze squares."

Hamid reached into his backpack for the gauze then watched as Ginny placed the plum in it. She held it over the boy's mouth and squeezed. Juice trickled in the boy's mouth.

"Go slowly," Angela cautioned.

The boy's throat moved spasmodically as he made reflexive swallowing movements.

"I have another one," Derrick said. "Do you want to try more?"

"Let's get him to the cave first," Hamid suggested looking up at the early evening sun. "It's getting late."

They were about to lift the canvas stretcher when the boy began coughing. He was conscious! He tried to sit up, only to weakly give up the task. They had all backed away at the first cough. Hamid now moved hesitantly forward. He squatted beside the makeshift stretcher in time to see the boy's eyes open again.

"You'll be okay," he said. "We are just trying to help you. You were stuck under a beam in one of the houses."

The boy eyed them nervously, then slowly nodded and closed his eyes again. "Many days..." he murmured. "Water?"

Using the same method Hamid supported his head and gave him more fruit juice.

He swallowed eagerly, finally lying back. His eyes were open once again.

"I'm Hamid."

"Dystaran."

"Desaran?"

"Name. Name Dystaran." The eyes flickered to the others. Fear entered his eyes again as he spotted Club.

"Don't worry," Hamid said. "He's tame. He won't hurt you." He motioned to the rest of his friends.

They moved forward and introduced themselves.

It was too much for Dystaran. After murmured thanks, his eyes closed.

Hamid decided to continue with the plan. They climbed back into the house's basement to get the boy's bow and arrows. They then loaded the weapons and as much of their supplies as they could onto the stretcher with Dystaran. Next they divided the rest of supplies. Four of them were needed to support the stretcher, but they rotated the chore for the trip. Dystaran opened his eyes briefly when they first lifted him; soon he either fell asleep or lapsed into unconsciousness for the rest of the journey back.

Lenny pulled Hamid away from the stretcher while Derrick, Ginny and Angela were switching places to take their turn at lifting. "Do you think we should let him see the cave?"

"We don't have much choice. Anyway, I now think that finding him may just help us survive. I am hoping he, or his people, will help us. We know nothing about living off the land and we're stuck here. It's summer now. What will we do come the winter?"

Lenny was silent.

"Home at last," Ginny called.

"Home?" Derrick looked from the mountain to Ginny, his look clearly questioning her sanity.

"This place grows on you," Lenny muttered.

Derrick grumbled his disagreement.

They had to lift Dystaran, fireman style, up to the cave's entrance. From there, Derrick and Lente left to collect fruits, while Lenny and Ginny tied one end of the rope to an iron pot and went back into the cave to see if they could lower it for water. Hamid stayed and watched as Angela dipped into his first-aid kit for disinfectant. The boy was conscious, and obviously in a lot of pain; he made no effort to speak.

Hamid was trying to figure out how to remove Dystaran's smelly clothes when Lenny and Ginny returned, bursting with excitement.

"We did it," Ginny shouted. "We got some water. Look! Now we can boil the potatoes and vegetables."

"Great," Derrick applauded mockingly, as he dumped the raincoat full of fruits on the ground. "We'll have a balanced diet. Fruits, veggies *and* water for dinner."

Other than making a face, Angela said nothing, and the others were equally resigned.

After using water to clean Dystaran's leg, Angela applied disinfectant then bandaged the leg. Next they fed Dystaran more fruit juice and some small pieces of fruit. Feeding seemed to help and Dystaran became more aware of his surroundings. He watched them as they ate.

He was so silent that they had almost forgotten about him until he abruptly asked. "Escape you too from the Trumen?"

They all turned to stare at him. What was he talking about?

"What?" Derrick voiced the only question in their minds.

Dystaran looked at them in turn. "You are no Truman."

They were still blank. He spoke English with a weird accent. Besides, he was using terms that made his English sound totally foreign.

"Truman?" Hamid asked. "What's that?"

Dystaran seemed too exhausted to answer. His eyes were closed again.

Hamid came and squatted next to him. "Listen. Try to get some sleep and tomorrow we'll sort things out. Do you understand me?"

The eyes opened again. "Understand tomorrow. Understand some."

Hamid grinned. Dystaran closed his eyes again and seemed to go to sleep.

"What does he mean by Truman?" Derrick asked.

"Ask him tomorrow," Hamid stretched. "I'm going to sleep."

"What if they come looking for him?" Lente looked around nervously as if expecting someone or something to jump out of the bushes. "He said he escaped. What if they find us?"

Lenny seriously considered the question – a welcome change. "Well, I don't think there are any Trumen or anybody around. He was in that house for days. If they were around, they would have found him."

Hamid stretched again. "Like I said, I'm for bed."

"Even if it takes one hundred pots of water, I am going to get a wash first," Angela announced.

"Me too," Ginny said.

"How about making the cave be the bathing room?" Lente asked. "We can fill the pots and wash in there."

"Good idea," Lenny said. "You three girls go ahead. We'll go next."

It took a few exhausting hours for them to all take baths and wash most of their clothes. They were even able to use the fire as a crude clothes dryer. Hamid thought they should offer to wash Dystaran since he was still smelly but couldn't work up the energy – tomorrow.

*****

Dystaran was much better the next day. With help, he washed and cleaned his clothes. His leg was still swollen, but he was able to hop about with the help of a tree branch. They allowed him only enough time to finish breakfast before the questions started.

"So, what happened to the people who lived in the houses?" Derrick began.

"All are dead." Dystaran said as he swallowed a bite of plum.

"We know that," Lenny said impatiently. "We want to know how they died and when."

Dystaran shrugged. "Ones no Trumen so die."

"There is that word again," Ginny said. "What is Trumen?"

"The Trumen. Live they on the island to the South. Manhattan."

"Manhattan!" Lente cried. "Manhattan is still here!"

"Just a minute," Hamid was close to banging his head in frustration. "You say all the people in these houses died because they aren't Trumen. Right?"

"Correct yes," Dystaran said. Then he asked his own question. "Escape you from the Trumen too?"

"No, we didn't escape…." Derrick began.

Hamid interrupted. "We sort of escaped. But we came from a place that is far, far from here."

Dystaran was excited. "Then others are no Trumen. Where live these others? Their help is much needed."

"Others like us, you mean?" Hamid struggled to understand. "What do the Trumen look like?"

Dystaran looked momentarily confused. "How possible that you no know the Trumen?"

Lenny gave Hamid a quick glance. "Where we come from there are no Trumen," he explained.

Dystaran was clearly excited and amazed. "Is it possible, you take me there?"

"Tell us about the Trumen," Hamid urged. "We'll talk

about where we came from later."

Dystaran looked ready to argue. Lenny forestalled him. "Look, we are totally lost. We're not even sure we can get back to where we came from. Tell us your story first."

Dystaran munched for a moment then decided. "Very tall are the Trumen. Very tall. One head…. Sometimes two heads taller than us. Rule they all the land. Until Scigam rules. Scigam was Abnorm, as is I."

"Abnorm?" Hamid asked.

Dystaran stopped chewing. He stared at the low fire. "The Trumen say we are no normal."

Again, Hamid stopped him. Dystaran's story was difficult to understand because of his strange speech patterns. "Okay. So far we know that most of the world's population was killed by someone or something and somehow only Trumen survived."

Dystaran nodded. "Many years ago, in all the lands lived Abnorms. They all died. The Trumen…."

"But what killed everybody?" Ginny almost shouted in her confusion. "Why did they die?"

Dystaran stared at her. "I am no sure," he admitted. "The Trumen say they were no normal and we will die also and soon." He hesitated, and then added. "Abnorms now live longer than Trumen. All Trumen die at young ages. Very young – maybe they have forty years, no more. At forty years Abnorms look much younger than the Trumen." He paused. "No one knows why it is the Trumen look so old at forty and why they die. No one can stop the death. It is very sad."

"But there were no Trumen living in the world." Derrick was equally confused. "So where did the first Truman come from?"

"They were the ones that did no die."

They all stared at each other. This made no sense!

"There were no Trumen where we came from," Lenny said definitely.

"Wait a second!" Angela was shaking her head. "If all Abnorms died, how come you are here?"

"Fifty years in the past, possible more, the first Abnorms were again born. They had the parents of Trumen. Even now the parents can be Trumen and one child Abnorm. My father, my mother, they are Trumen…. It is no known why this is so."

"That's not right," Derrick protested. "I tell you there were no Trumen…."

Again, Hamid interrupted. "Let's hear the rest of Dystaran's story before trying to poke holes in it."

"What is this poke hole?"

"Where we come from, that's how we say, question," Lenny said.

"Ah. Question means the same as poke hole."

His response was not quite right, but Hamid nodded, impatient to continue. He began ticking off on his finger. "First everyone dies except Trumen – we don't know where they came from. Next, Trumen take over the world, but then some Trumen parents start having Abnorm babies. And Abnorms are people like you and me. Right?"

Dystaran nodded.

"So, tell us, what happened after your guy was made leader?"

Dystaran sighed. "Scigam was stupid. He wished to control. When it is known that the Abnorms live much longer than the Trumen, he tries to put only Abnorms on the Supreme Liberty. He also arrested or killed any Trumen who would disagree with him. The Trumen come to hate Scigam and all Abnorms. They say we are diseased and to have children with us will be to poison future generations of all the people. Two summers ago, the Supreme Liberty that Scigam formed is declared illegal by a group of Trumen. All on the Supreme Liberty are killed and the Trumen started a new Supreme Liberty. Immediately they pass a new law – all ones no Trumen are no normal and must be killed or imprisoned. As it was in the past, so it must be again."

"There was a coup," Lenny said in amusement.

Derrick glared at him. "I hope you'll be laughing when they come after you."

Dystaran gave them a quick confused glance before continuing, quietly. "It is with the help of my parents that I escaped. They are Trumen and so are my brother and sister, so they remain in Manhattan. I..." he paused before continuing. "It was very dark the night. The brother of my mother came to warn us. Almost he was too late. There was a pounding on the front door as we slipped out the back."

"You mean the Trumen tried to wipe out all Abnorms?" Ginny was aghast, as she finally understood what Dystaran really meant.

Dystaran nodded. "Scigam and many Abnorms are killed. Very few escaped. Almost, they succeed to kill all." Dystaran said grimly.

"But how do they know who is who?" Derrick asked. "How do they know Abnorms from Trumen? I mean, don't you ever have a short Trumen?"

Hamid stood up. He was a good head taller than Dystaran. "Are the Trumen taller than me?"

Dystaran looked him up and down then hesitated. "Very tall are the Trumen. Maybe as tall as you are tall." He tried to explain further. "When a Truman is the age of ten, he looks the age of the Abnorm at age twenty. A Truman at thirty is like the Abnorm at fifty."

"I know!" Angela spoke up excitedly. "There is a disease like that." She looked at the others. "Well, I don't really know if it is a disease. I think it may be a sort of genetic thing. When someone has it, they age faster than normal people. Maybe that is what the Trumen have."

"That makes more sense," Ginny mused. "Everybody in the world got a deadly disease and those who survived were left with a new disease that caused them to age faster than normal."

Hamid nodded. "I think that is what happened. The few people who survived then called themselves Trumen."

"And what's happening now is that things are returning to normal and normal people are being born again." Derrick finished.

"The Abnorms," Lenny grinned. "People without the disease."

Dystaran had watched and listened carefully throughout this exchange. "Explain to me this disease you speak of."

Hamid abruptly decided to confide in him. Taking turns, they told Dystaran their story. "So, you see we really are lost."

Dystaran stared at them. "It is like a dream, your story," he admitted.

"So do you believe us?" Angela asked.

Again, he looked at them carefully. "Yes." He hesitated. "Your words are different. And the dress on you is different. Also, that." He pointed to their watches. "And this is a strange light." He touched Lenny's flashlight. "It is a strange story, but it is I believe."

Lenny grinned at him. "So you see, we need your help.

There is not much we can do to help you."

At that Dystaran looked grim. "The Trumen are trying to kill us all. Two summers ago, very few were the Abnorms who escaped the death and left Manhattan. The Trumen did no follow. Now many parents try to save their Abnorm children. When the Supreme Liberty finds a child is Abnorm, the child is always killed. When a child reaches two or three years it is possible to tell if the child will be Truman or Abnorm so the parent will bring the children to us. It is so that our village is growing. Our problem now is that the Trumen do no want this."

"So the Trumen are hunting you." Hamid concluded.

Dystaran nodded. "They no want our village to get bigger. I think one day soon they will even attack our village. "

"Did they attack you?" Ginny asked. "Is that what happened to you? I mean, is that how you got in the houses?"

"There were three of us. We had collected two children – there is a meeting spot. Not long after we collect the children, we saw that two Trumen follow us. We do no want to lead them to our village, so we go in a different direction pass our village. We also separate to trick them. It is then that they follow me. I try to hide in the houses. When the sun is down, I try to get out. It is then that I trip and the wood fall on my leg. I cannot move, and I am afraid to call out." He shrugged. "So, I had to stay the night. The next day I try again to free the leg, but I cannot. For two days I stay.... Or maybe three.... I do no remember."

There was a short silence.

"You were more than lucky that we came by," Lenny finally said, perfectly imitating Dystaran's speech pattern.

Dystaran grinned. "Yes. I thank you. I was more than lucky." He seemed to especially enjoy Lenny's mimicry.

"How far away do your friends live?" Hamid asked.

"Just more than one day."

"Do you want to go back now, or wait until you are stronger?"

"You help me, we go now."

"No," Angela objected. "You can't do much walking on that leg now. Maybe in one day. You have to rest your leg."

"And we can't leave here," Lente added.

"We can't survive here on our own Lente." Hamid was serious. "We need their help."

"Sounds more like they need ours," Lenny muttered.

"But what if...." After a quick glance at Dystaran, Ginny hesitated. "I mean.... Should we leave here? These Trumen may have some terrible disease and we may get it."

"I think it's more like we will give them a disease," Angela said. "Besides we've already met Dystaran. If we're going to get anything, we've already got it."

"Reassuring, isn't she?" Derrick muttered.

"Do you want to hear lies instead of the truth," Hamid challenged.

"I still don't think we should leave here," Lente tried to change the subject.

"So," Hamid was still annoyed with Derrick's verbal attack on Angela. "Are you going to eat fruits and drink water for the rest of your life?"

"But if we leave here," Lente asked, "How will we ever be able to get back home?"

"If we stay here, we are likely to die of starvation," Lenny said flatly.

"Or of cold," Hamid was a little calmer. "What are we going to do come winter?"

Dystaran had listened carefully to the swift exchange. He now interrupted. "If it is your wish to stay here, I could show you how to make the bow and arrow so that you can get meat. Also, I would show you how to use the skins of the deer or the bear for winter covering."

Derrick was distracted. "Bears! There are bears in these woods?"

Dystaran nodded. "Many animals. There are the bears, the deer, the coyote and even the wolves. Also, there are many wild dogs and cats; even sometimes we see the moose. You will no starve."

"Moose!" Ginny exclaimed. "Moose and bears in the Bronx!"

Dystaran nodded.

"And wild dogs?" Angela shuddered. "Don't tell me you eat dogs?"

Dystaran grinned. "No. We do no eat the dogs. The dogs can be very vicious. You must keep a watch on Club. It is easy for the wild dogs to kill him."

"Thanks, Dystaran." Hamid looked over at Club. The dog had raised his head at hearing his name. He was safe for now. Next, Hamid looked at the others. Derrick looked resigned. Lenny wore his normal amused look. The girls all looked worried. "We cannot stay here," he decided. "We have to leave."

Chapter 6

It was four days before Dystaran was fit enough to travel. They used the time to learn from each other. Dystaran used his bow and arrow to catch a deer on the second day. He showed them how to remove the skin of the animal without damaging it. He then scraped the skin – they also scraped the skin of the coyote that they had eaten on the first day although their coyote's skin was damaged and nowhere near as good as the deer's skin. Dystaran's people used animal skins for winter coverings and for clothes. With Dystaran's, help Derrick was able to whittle a spear, make three bows and a bunch of arrows. Unfortunately, these arrows were not metal tipped as were Dystaran's. In exchange for the survival lessons, they showed Dystaran their watches and flashlights – he was fascinated by them – and the few other things they had. They also told him about life in their world.

The Trumen had lost a lot of knowledge. Cars and electricity were foreign to them. Houses were made of wood or red brick. All the abandoned houses and apartments were excellent sources of red brick. Red brick was also used to pave streets and wood was used for cooking and heating. Transportation was by horses, horse-drawn carriages, or by boat. As a child, Dystaran had traveled as far north as Connecticut by boat.

Apart from the Trumen of Manhattan and the Abnorms of his village, Dystaran knew of three other communities, one in Long Island, one in New Jersey and the one he had visited in Connecticut. He admitted that there were lots more. Those communities probably traded with others and all the communities were peopled by Trumen.

Abnorm births had appeared in the other communities at about the same time they appeared in Manhattan. However, all Abnorms were also killed off at about the same time as well. Dystaran's father in Manhattan was their only means of passing or getting information about the other Trumen communities, and Dystaran knew of no other village of Abnorms or even if other Abnorms had escaped the wipe-out.

With time on their hands, they explored the abandoned houses for information and for supplies. What they couldn't figure out was the actual year. Dystaran called it 286, which meant nothing to them. That was a Truman creation. They started counting from the year a guy who organized the first Truman village was born.

"You know what's so strange about this?" Lenny was prying open an old 'fridge. He and Hamid were searching through one of the houses. The girls were at camp with Club, and Dystaran and Derrick were hunting food.

"What?" Hamid asked as he concentrated on opening what looked like a fire safe.

"There is no sign of life. I mean.... These people didn't die here. They left. There are no skeletons – no bones. There aren't any cars in the middle of the street. There are few cars parked at the curb and even fewer cars in garages."

"You think whatever it was, happened over a period of time?"

"I don't know what to think."

"They were probably evacuated. You know, like when you read about natural disasters. The government evacuates the people. I think that's what happened."

"So where did the people go?"

Hamid shrugged. He could only deal with one problem at a time. "Wherever they went, they are now dead so what does it matter." He finally got the safe open. "Hey look! Records!"

The safe documented the births, marriages and achievements of a family called Hoftin.

"Look!" Hamid pulled out a crumbling paper. "It says here that Teddy Hoftin got married in 2029 to Lindy Reiber."

Lenny leaned over. "Let me see that."

The papers were brittle with age, literally dissolving as the boys handled them. The last date on any of the records was 2079.

Hamid sighed as he sat up. "So now we know that sometime – probably after 2079 – something or someone caused a disease that wiped out most of the world's population."

Lenny nodded. "They left these papers behind. So that means they were planning on coming back."

"Like I said, they were evacuated."

"Maybe they died before they could return."

"Could be," Hamid said as he stretched. He really didn't see what difference it made. "My back is killing me from all this bending. I say we go back to the camp now."

Lenny looked at the evening sun and reluctantly agreed. "I want to come back and explore some more."

Three days later, after more searching by Derrick and Lenny, they were no closer to figuring out what year it was. They all agreed that two or even three hundred years could have passed since the people who lived here had left or were forced to leave. Not that they could prove the time. They did get some clues as to what caused the people to abandon their houses. They collected scraps of newspapers and bits and pieces of papers, even other records. From the newspapers they learned that much of the world as they knew it was under some sort of quarantine. Governments were trying to control the spread of a manmade virus that was deliberately let loose in major cities. It took a month after exposure to the virus before the first flu-like symptoms began to appear, but after that death came quickly. Usually within days of the first symptoms, the patient began bleeding internally and soon all the organs of the body simply stopped functioning. There was no known cure, and the death rate was close to 100%.

"I guess the quarantine didn't work," Lenny muttered as he looked up from reading the newspaper scraps.

It was late evening, and they were at camp sorting through the mass of papers and supplies they had collected.

Hamid looked thoughtful. "I guess not."

"Both the entire world!" Ginny was shaking her head in disbelief. "That virus must have wiped out the population of the entire world."

"Except for the Trumen," Angela reminded her. "The people who survived became the Trumen."

"Shirts!" Lenny's mockery of Derrick's favorite expression said it all.

*****

It was finally time to go. With Dystaran's help they had all fashioned backpacks of woven leaves and young branches to carry supplies. Hamid also carried his original backpack. Dystaran explained that, after crossing the river to the Bronx, his people followed an old train track until they found a large area of relatively flat land, suitable for farming. Hamid soon realized that the train tracks that Dystaran spoke of was the elevated Number Two line, which made him suspect that the large area of cleared land was the former Bronx Botanical Gardens.

He was sure he was right. They were traveling due south, in single file, along what was once White Plains Road. Dystaran led the way, followed by Ginny and Lenny, then Lente and Derrick. Angela, Hamid and Club were last in line.

Lente kept giving the overhead train tracks – or what was left of them – apprehensive looks. "What if they fall on us?"

Derrick, who was behind her, looked up. Some sections of the train tracks had fallen to the ground and were now entirely covered with undergrowth. Those were the safe parts. The danger came from what was left. In some areas, sections hung precariously, supported by crumbling columns of concrete.

"I don't think they are going anywhere," Hamid said. Nevertheless, he called to Dystaran. "Isn't there any other way to your village?"

"No that I know."

Since he could do nothing about that particular fear, Hamid focused on his other concern. He frowned as he watched Lente and Derrick. They were getting too close. He didn't mind Derrick as a friend for himself, but he was not sure he wanted him as a friend for his sister. Maybe he could talk to Lente in private tonight. Well…. Maybe not tonight. They were going to keep watch tonight. Talking to

Lente would mean giving up Angela as his watch partner. No. Definitely not tonight!

He decided to stick with simple problems first. "Watch where you put your feet," he now warned. "There are metal pieces from the track on the ground as well."

There were really no distinct trails, but the going was not too bad since they were traveling on what was once a road. The real hazard was that they were hemmed in by the remains of the tracks on their left and by crumbling apartment buildings on their right. Hamid kept a firm grip on Club. He had even fashioned a leash with his rope. Yes, he had actually cut the rope, since he was afraid Club would wander off and get injured, or even bark and bring down one of the buildings on them.

It was late evening, their first day away from the cave, when they turned west and left the train tracks. What a relief! After a few more minutes of trekking, the woods came to an abrupt end.

"Wow!" Ginny exclaimed. "What a view!" The road, or what passed for a road, had ended with a sheer drop at what was apparently supposed to be an overpass, but was now a huge gorge.

"I think that used to be the Bronx River Parkway." Lenny pointed to the remains of the highway below.

The highway had actually defeated the woods. True the overpass had fallen onto it, in a huge mass of twisted metal and concrete, but the length of the highway – and they could see stretches of it in both directions – was relatively clear. There were shrubs yes, and numerous small plants – even a few trees, but not the thick woods that they had just emerged from. The tightly packed surface of the original roadway had somehow managed to starve off the woods.

"How are we going to cross?" Derrick asked as they stood and looked down at the highway. He absently patted Club as the dog squeezed in front of him.

Dystaran grinned. "The one only way. We climb."

"That's what I was afraid you'd say," Derrick grumbled.

"There the climb will no be too bad," Dystaran pointed to an area north of where they were standing.

Ginny looked. It was a gentler slope, but still a slope. "I'm dead on my feet. Couldn't we camp here for the night?"

Suddenly a shot rang out.

"Get down!" Dystaran screamed.

They dropped to the ground and began scrambling back into the woods.

"What was that?" Hamid kept a firm grip on Club's collar as he crawled up to Dystaran.

"Trumen!" There was a grim look on Dystaran's face.

Derrick crawled over to them. "Shirts!" he muttered. "Where?"

Dystaran looked confused. "Shirts?" he repeated.

Hamid gave a muffled laugh. "That's Derrick's favorite curse word. Ignore him."

"Oh," Dystaran face cleared up. He pointed. "They may be over there. Beyond the gorge. The Trumen have the guns – many guns. We have few. It is maybe that they wait for us."

"You mean they are trying to ambush us." Ginny was more amazed than scared as she crawled up beside Lenny.

"Ambush?" Dystaran did not understand the word.

"The Trumen," Derrick explained. "Are they waiting? In the woods on the other side? "

"Yes. I think. It is this way to our village," Dystaran

added. "Always, we use this path."

"So what do we do now?" Hamid asked. "Is there another way?"

"There is no a way that I know," Dystaran said. "Perhaps in the night we could go quietly down the gorge and pass them."

There was silence. No one liked the idea of creeping pass men with guns – especially not in the dark.

"If only we had guns too, then we'd be even," Derrick muttered.

"Sure," Lenny dripped sarcasm. "Let's go buy some at the corner store."

Ginny gave Lenny an irritated glare.

Angela turned to Dystaran. "How did the Trumen know we were coming this way?"

Nobody could come up with an answer.

"What are you getting at?" Hamid asked.

Angela hesitated. "I mean.... Could it be your people, Dystaran? Maybe they are keeping watch."

Dystaran frowned. "It could be so," he admitted. "But my people would no shoot at us."

"They may not know it's you," Hamid said. "They were expecting one person and we are a group of seven."

"Okay, let's have a volunteer," Lenny grinned. "Raise your hand if you want to go over and show the guy shooting your ID. This is not the time to act wimpy. We... ouch!"

Ginny had jabbed him in the ribs with her elbow. "Shut up!"

"Serves you right," Derrick said as Lenny glared. Lente began giggling.

Hamid gave a long-suffering sigh before sitting up and removing his backpack. He searched through the pocket compartment.

"What are you looking for?" Angela asked.

"My map. You may be right about the guy or guys shooting, but we can't take any chances. I have another idea." He pulled out his map, opening up the section of the Bronx, and spread it on the ground. "Listen for a minute. Since we started, I've been checking directions. It's easy to tell where the streets were because remains of the houses are still there. I think right now we're here. We turned off White Plains Road onto Pelham Parkway."

The others sat or knelt as they peered over his shoulder. Dystaran was fascinated by the map and could not stop asking questions.

"So, all we got to do is travel on the highway to the next exit."

In a break in the questions, Hamid traced the path with a finger. "That should take us right to the Gardens."

They digested this theory.

"So how do we find this exit?" Lenny finally asked. "Do we check the road signs?"

Hamid ignored the sarcasm. "If we walk close to the edge of the highway, we should be able to find it. It would be the least wooded area."

Derrick had been staring intently at his toes. He now looked up. "And what do you imagine those guys with guns are going to do when they see us walking along the highway?"

Hamid thought a bit. "They'll never see us in the dark – they can't." He looked up. "It's not a full moon so we should be okay, especially if we keep close to the edge of the woods. And best of all we don't even have to use any light. We can't get lost on the highway."

"Explain again to me this plan. I no understand."

Dystaran had been listening intently.

Hamid quickly explained. Dystaran was nodding excitedly even before he finished. "Yes.... Yes. It is a good plan."

"But..." Ginny was still not certain she liked the plan. "Will we find the next exit in the dark?"

"We can do that tomorrow. What we need to do now is get away from this spot without getting lost in the dark."

Again, there was silence.

"We'll have to wait until dark to start moving, right?" Lenny was wearing a remarkable serious expression.

Hamid nodded.

"Okay." Lenny started to stand, and then changed his mind as he remembered the men with guns. "We'll go for it."

"Good." Hamid leaned back against a tree trunk. "Let's settle down now. We needn't go down the gorge here. When it gets dark we'll walk further up, then climb down. Club will warn us if they come any closer."

"When I think how we were just standing there." Ginny shivered. "They could have just killed us all."

"We are far away," Dystaran said. "Guns cannot shoot very great distance. They no could kill us. It was stupid that they shoot. Now we know that they hide."

"We are so *so* lucky one of them was stupid," Ginny said.

"And that they don't have guns like in our world." Derrick turned to Dystaran. "Where we come from, they have guns that could have picked us off one-by-one even from this distance."

They began telling Dystaran more about their world as they waited for dark.

"I hope they sit on that hill top for days waiting for

us," Lenny said as they finally prepared to move.

"Shh.... Shh," Hamid said.

Lente giggled.

"Quiet!" Hamid covered her mouth.

After walking some distance parallel to the highway, they slid down the slope. It was an easy slope, but Derrick and Lenny still had to help Dystaran to steady himself. In a matter of minutes, they were on their way and they made sure to turn a corner before making camp. In no time, they were stuffing down a dinner of water, fruits, vegetables, and leftover deer meat. Tired and full they soon settled for the night. Angela and Hamid had first watch. Before going to bed, Angela checked Dystaran's leg. It was doing fine, but he would need his stick crutches another day to avoid putting too much pressure on the leg.

*****

They were up early the next day. The highway meandered along, never far from the river. It was an opportunity they could not pass up. Since leaving their real homes there hadn't been any means to get a decent wash. So, although the sun was not quite up and the air was fresh and invigorating, they all tumbled into the water, even Club – clothes and all.

"Wow!" Lente screamed. "It's freezing!"

"Keep your voice down," Hamid warned. "Sounds carry in the early morning."

They tried, they really did, but it was hard to keep quiet. After a good hour of healthy splashing passed, and with their skin prune-like, they finally, reluctantly, climbed out. By noon the hot sun had dried them out. They were no longer wet, but hunger became their pressing need. Before long, they came across a small herd of deer. The animals were grazing on the young plants that dotted the highway. Hamid quickly covered Club's mouth, to prevent him from warning the animals, then gave his dog a stern command. Reassured that Club would keep still, he, Derrick and Lenny took out their brand-new bows and arrows. Dystaran began giving quick instructions.

Whoosh.... Whoosh.... Whoosh.... It was disgusting! They all missed! In the next second the frightened animals were gone.

The boys stood scowling at the fleeing deer. Club started barking and Lente stifled a laugh. "Next time, let Dystaran try," she suggested.

Immediately, three scowls were directed at her.

"Well, that was supposed to be breakfast," she said defensively. That morning they ate fruits, but nothing else. The vegetables were all gone. So was the meat.

"The only way we'll get better at this is to practice," Derrick pointed out.

"Practice on the trees," was Angela's suggestion.

"Yeah," Ginny agreed. "There are enough of them. And best of all you don't have to worry about your target running away."

"That's the point," Lenny was impatient. "We need to practice on moving targets."

"Not when I'm hungry you don't."

"Now look here..." Lenny began.

"Okay.... Okay," Hamid interrupted them. "It's too early to start a stupid argument."

"He is just grumpy 'cause he missed," Ginny teased.

"Well you needn't rub it in."

"Ouch," Ginny grinned, "another grumpy one."

Hamid pulled out his map, deliberately ignoring her. "According to my map, the next exit should be somewhere around here. We took this corner last night." He pointed.

*****

As Hamid had predicted, finding the exit proved easy. Soon they were wandering along what used to be the road to the Bronx Botanical Gardens

"Recognize anything?" Derrick asked Dystaran – for the third time.

"How can he, with you bugging him every few minutes?" Lenny glowered.

"Children.... Children." Ginny was grinning.

Hamid ignored them both and checked his compass again. "Well, we're still in the general area of the Gardens."

"Ahh...." Dystaran face suddenly broke into a broad grin as they came up a rise. "This place I know." Taking the lead once again he took them away from the thinly wooded road and back into the deep woods. "There is a trail here that often we use."

The six followed him in silence. Soon they came to a well-worn trail that was wide enough for them to walk two abreast. After a while, Hamid cleared his throat and asked.

"Dystaran. What are your people like?"

"Like?"

"Like as in – will they kill us, throw us in jail or what?" Lenny stopped. He was frowning. "We should have asked before."

"I wondered what race they'd be," Ginny said as they all stopped.

Derrick nodded in agreement. "So what race are they?"

"Race?" Dystaran was clearly mystified.

"Do they look more like me or like Lenny?" Hamid asked.

Dystaran looked at them both. "Some Abnorms are as you are and some are as Lenny is."

The six stared at each other. It was obvious that Dystaran did not understand the concept of race. Was that good or bad? The uncertainty was raising their anxiety level.

"Let's move on." Hamid finally muttered. "We'll find out soon enough."

"I do no understand," Dystaran was still puzzled. "Why think you that my people will harm you?"

"Never mind us," Lenny said. He took a deep breath. "We're just running scared."

Dystaran grinned. "You will be more than safe," he promised.

They nodded, but no one felt like commenting.

In less than half an hour they were at his village. Decision time! They were intruders in this world; would Dystaran's people accept them, enslave them or kill them?

Chapter 7

Almost the entire village came out to greet them. While they were exclaiming over Dystaran and listening to his story – they had obviously believed him dead – Hamid got a chance to look around.

The village consisted of three huge log cabins in the center, roughly surrounded by about thirty small wooden huts. The land was flat, with few trees to obstruct the view. More than likely they had cut down the trees to build the cabins. Beyond the cabins it was obvious that farming was the Abnorms' major food source. There were also some separate, fenced areas of small animals. These were some distance away and Hamid could not be sure what animals were kept. However, it was not the animals that caught and held his attention. It was the amazing mix of the people. In his world he had never come across such diversity. Some like Dystaran had an olive complexion with dark hair and eyes. Yet others had blond and even red hair. Eye colors ran the range from deep blue through green to black. There were bewildering combinations that did not fit what he was accustomed to. Those with dark skin sometimes had blond hair or even blue eyes. Caucasian facial features and skin color were mixed with black hair texture even when the hair color was blond.

The mixture left Hamid's mind reeling. His friends were also blinking in confusion. Now they understood why Dystaran hadn't commented on their race!

Having greeted Dystaran, the Abnorms now turned to the strangers.

Dystaran introduced them.

"Treber is the brother of my mother," he said as a tall man came forward. "He is leader of our village."

Treber was about forty years old and looked to be the oldest Abnorm in the village. He, like most of the adult males in the village, wore what could pass for pants, but left his chest bare. His hair was jet black, worn straight to his shoulders. As he smiled, Hamid and his friends were still trying to absorb his curious blend of features. His eyes were violet blue, a sharp contrast to his honey brown complexion.

"Welcome," he said. "I can no thank you enough for the rescue of my sister's son. Come! You are tired. My two daughters will help you."

He led them to the main cabin – the one in the very center. Along the way, other Abnorms came up to introduce themselves and hear the story of Dystaran's rescue. A surprise greeted them at the cabin. Treber's wife and three children, a son and two daughters were Trumen.

"My wife, Garoci," Treber pointed to a slight Oriental looking woman who was cooking over an open fire. Garoci smiled. She looked about sixty years old! "And my daughters, Stadi and Subini." The girls were sewing. They both had their father's complexion, but their mother's features and brown eye color. Both also had the straight brown hair of their mother. They both looked up, yet neither smiled. Treber turned around. "Where went Fasraben?"

"I am here father." Fasraben looked an older version of his father. He was actually balding! He entered the room slowly and gave Dystaran an expressionless stare. "Good.

You escaped them," he said without any visible emotion.

Dystaran did not seem to find anything usual in Fasraben's behavior. He just grinned. "Many thanks to my new friends," he said, before launching into his explanations yet again. To Hamid and friends, he continued. "Fasraben was with me the day the Trumen followed us."

Later that night as Hamid settled into bed – the beds were made of straw – he turned to Lenny. "What do you think?"

They were lying in the dark, in the boys' cabin. Because there were so many abandoned children, the village had set up separate quarters for them. The other large cabin in the center of the village was the girls' cabin. The children were cared for by the entire village, but only one adult usually slept in the children's cabins at nights. Married couples, and a few older men and women lived in the smaller surrounding cabins, while Treber and his family, including Dystaran, lived in the main center cabin.

"Think about what?" Derrick asked from his other side.

Hamid glanced around. Silence at last! These boys were very friendly and had chatted them nearly to death before succumbing to sleep. He, Lenny and Derrick were the oldest 'children' in the room. Here, boys their age were already married.

Lenny stirred. "Ginny and the others must feel even weirder than we do. Girls marry at ten or eleven."

"At twelve," Hamid kept his voice low to avoid waking any of the young boys. "In Manhattan they married at nine, but since coming here they passed a new law. Dystaran told me."

Derrick mused. "Dystaran say Trumen girls marry

early because they age so much faster than Abnorms."

Hamid's voice went even lower. "He told me that he is soon to marry his cousin."

Lenny snorted, "Which one?"

"Stadi. Believe it or not she is only fifteen."

"That's just creepy!" Derrick muttered. "I feel sorry for him. Even my mom looks younger."

Hamid continued. "Well, he doesn't seem to mind. These people are very accepting of differences in others. He told me she was married before. Her husband died before they left Manhattan."

"How come Subini isn't married," Derrick asked.

"She is only ten."

"Ten! She looks older than we are!" Lenny exclaimed. "And imagine! Fasraben is only a year older than Dystaran. I wonder why he isn't married?"

"Maybe none of the Abnorm girls want him," Hamid muttered, remembering Fasraben's cool greeting. Apart from Treber's family, there were only two other Trumen in the village, a man and a young boy. There were no other Trumen girls or women.

With a grin in his voice, Lenny murmured, "I know the feeling. Talk about cold. He could freeze an icicle."

"It is not just looks you know. I think they are old – mentally. That's probably Farasben's problem. He's supposed to be the child, but he feels and looks older than his own father. Did you see that other man – Sergin?"

"Yeah," Lenny said. "He is supposed to be twenty-five. He acts and looks like he's about fifty."

Derrick changed the subject. "At least we know that the Trumen haven't found this village."

"Yeah, Angela was partly right after all." Hamid's voice reflected his satisfaction. "The men shooting just

Abnorms out hunting."

"Yeah, but there's something I still don't understand," Derrick continued his train of thought. "How did the Trumen know the children's pickup point? They were able to track Dystaran from there."

"Do you think there's a spy here?" Lenny asked.

"Maybe not here," Hamid said, "But definitely in Manhattan. Someone told the Trumen the time and place."

"Dystaran is afraid they killed his father," Derrick said. "His father was the person arranging the children's pickup point."

"These Abnorms will have to do something – and soon." Hamid said. "The next time there may be a dozen Trumen waiting instead of only two."

"And the Trumen will find here soon," Lenny sounded positive. "The Abnorms are not even posting guards. A look how easy it was to find another way here. If they can follow Dystaran all the way up to where we were, they'll find this village."

They were both right, Hamid knew it. Worse, protecting this village would be next to impossible. Not only was it on a wide-open plain, with numerous entry points, there were only a handful of men capable of defending the village. And he didn't see any sign of any serious preparation to resist an attack.

*****

Within a short time, they had settled comfortably into village life. The boys adopted the bloomers-type shorts as worn by Dystaran, and the girls all got long tunic-looking dresses. Treber and his family were the only ones told the true story of where they came from. Others were told they had wandered south from the Northern regions after their village was destroyed. And they were the only survivors. The story was shaky, and Hamid wasn't sure how many people really believed it. What mattered was that although they initially felt like intruders, they were soon accepted. He was still amazed with the unconditional acceptance offered by the villagers. Hamid and his friends were never excluded from the family style living that the villagers practiced.

He also loved the fact that although Treber was the leader, the village was wholly democratic. In meetings, any adult could voice an opinion, and no one seemed to see race as an issue or discriminate against any individual based on their race. They were too mixed a group and had suffered enough because they were different from the ruling Trumen. The entire Abnorm village – it was just called the Village – had only 256 people, now 262. However, more than three-quarter of the village's population were children under the age of ten, and many of these children were under the age of five. Listening to their stories, and hearing of the family members left behind was really depressing. Worse was realizing that there was nothing that they could do to change the situation.

There was no organized form of learning in the village so within two weeks Ginny and Lente started a school. Their greatest need was paper. They had none and both girls began trying to figure out how to make paper from the abundant supply of wood. In the meantime, they were unbelievably patient with the younger children. The older ones had to work on the community farms surrounding the village but attended school whenever they could. In Manhattan, children attended school only to the age of eight for girls and ten for boys. Very few boys – only those who showed extraordinary abilities – attended further specialized schooling.

Angela began helping Sergin, the village healer. He was a Hispanic looking man with an extensive knowledge of herbal medicines, learned from his mother. And, although he was Truman, he had joined the Abnorms when they fled Manhattan because his son was Abnorm. His wife had died years ago and unfortunately, his son had not survived that initial flight from Manhattan, but Sergin had no reason to go back.

Derrick, along with another Abnorm, Gamnic, became busy with woodworking projects. They were bent on furnishing the entire village. Gamnic was the only person in the entire village who did not look mixed race. He had blond hair and a pale complexion that burned rather than tanned. Hamid became concerned enough to start warning him to avoid the sun. These people knew nothing about skin cancer.

Lenny wanted to make living in the village more comfortable. His biggest project was devising better mechanical tools for farming and he soon started combined projects with Derrick and Gamnic. Lenny however, was often frustrated because of the lack of metal. They should be tons of metal in the abandoned buildings. The problem was getting the raw material. That was when the problem got to Hamid's attention.

Hamid figured that with Fordham Road close by, they had a good chance of picking out the necessary supplies from the rubble of abandoned buildings. He had been working with Treber to map the area, trying to sort out their best plan of defense, maybe even find a more secure location for the village. However, searching for supplies seemed much more exciting. With Treber's approval he,

Lenny, Derrick, Dystaran, Fasraben, Gamnic, the three girls and three other Abnorms began planning the trip to Fordham Road. Hamid had tried, really tried, to convince the girls to stay in the village. They refused. Not that they were afraid of the Abnorms in the village; their fear was that somehow the boys would get back to the right time period, leaving them behind. That's how it came that, four weeks after first entering the Abnorm village, they unpacked their own clothes and were on their way out again.

The younger Abnorms recognized Fasraben as their leader, but Hamid became the unofficial leader of the group since they needed his maps and compass. He tried to stay on the former roads; that way they did not waste time hacking a path through the thick woods. Fasraben walked beside him or behind him when the paths did not allow two abreast. It was annoying. Hamid wanted to walk with Angela but found it virtually impossible to shake off Fasraben. The Truman questioned him, every step of the way, and wanted to know exactly how to use the maps and the compass. Once or twice Hamid had to bite his tongue to hold back a rude reply. And Lenny's permanent expression of unholy amusement only served to frustrate Hamid more. It took a full day and a half to reach Fordham Road – the most aggravating period in Hamid's life.

*****

Fordham Road, where they were standing, was lightly wooded. They surveyed what used to be one of the busiest shopping strips in the Bronx in amazement. Because the road went uphill with a curve, the dense woods did not totally limit their view. Not that there was much to see.

Here at the foot of the hill, stores – barely visible through the trees – were just crumbled heaps of rubble.

"Do we explore now or wait?" Lenny asked.

Lente wiped her brow. "I'm tired."

Hamid gave her a quick look. She looked exhausted. "It's getting late anyway and climbing through those buildings will be dangerous. Let's make camp here. Tomorrow we can start."

They didn't need convincing. Lente was not the only one tired. Within minutes they had a fire going, and a delicious stew was boiling. They had taken food for two days – mostly potatoes and carrots – since they figured they would be able to catch their meat. Yesterday they had caught two squirrels, but no large animal, so they were now short of meat.

"We have need to get more animal meat tomorrow," Fasraben commented as he sank his teeth into his squirrel's leg.

Dystaran and Gamnic nodded. Hamid had noticed that they almost always agreed with Fasraben. He scooped up a mouthful of stew with his wooded spoon and chewed thoughtfully. "If..." he began, then jerked around to stare into the dark woods that surrounded them."What was that?"

The howling sounded again.

Fasraben and the Abnorms were now the only ones calmly eating.

Dystaran shrugged. "It is possible a wild dog."

Angela was not convinced. "Are you sure it's not a wolf?"

Fasraben gave her an expressionless stare, "Wolf no. It sounds no like a wolf. Dystaran is correct. It is a wild dog that is howling." He paused. "It is rare that they attack yet they can be a danger. We must take care."

"He sounds so positive, you'd think he went into the woods to check," Lenny muttered to no one in particular.

Hamid hid a grin, although he felt that Lenny really should keep quiet. Fasraben was a pain, but his fear was that Fasraben would blow up. And if there was going to be a blow up, he would rather it didn't happen when they were miles away from the village.

"Are you sure they won't attack us?" Lente now asked as she looked around fearfully.

"They will no attack," Fasraben said. He was staring at Lenny – expressionlessly.

Hamid did not notice the exchange until a dull red blush started in Lenny's cheeks. Quickly, he grabbed Lenny's arm. Just what he didn't need – a staring war.

Lenny pulled his arm away, but the distraction was enough to break the staring match. After giving Hamid a glare, he began rubbing his arm as if Hamid's grip had really hurt. Hamid knew it hadn't. A quick glance at Fasraben left him exasperated. Fasraben was still staring at Lenny! What's wrong with him? Hamid looked across at Ginny, silently asking for her help. She was the only other person to notice the exchange. Ginny now moved from where she stood serving to sit beside Lenny. Hamid gave her a grateful look.

"I don't like this spot," Derrick muttered as he now looked around. "It is too open."

Fasraben turned to give *him* a stare.

Hamid welcomed the diversion. "Well, we can't strike it lucky two nights in a row," he said.

Last night they had found a good camping spot with their backs to a mountain of rocks. Here, an attack could come from any direction.

"We can protect ourselves with more fires," Fasraben said. It was not a suggestion. Gamnic and Dystaran and the other Abnorms immediately got up to get more firewood.

"Good idea," Hamid nodded, smothering a grin. Fasraben sure had them well-trained, he thought. "Also, Club will warn us if anything comes close."

Soon they had four fires going – one at each corner of a rough square. They felt a little safer as they settled down for the night. As before, they paired off with partners and set up a schedule so each pair would get a turn at keeping watch. There were nine males, so it was decided that the girls did not need to keep watch.

The next morning, they went straight to the buildings.

"Remember what happened to Dystaran," Hamid warned as Derrick started to climb into one of the buildings.

Fasraben eyed the crumbling remains of the two-story clothing store. "It would be good if the entire building came down. Now, it would no be wise to climb in."

"But how will we get the building to come down," Lente asked as she looked around.

"An earthquake would help," Lenny suggested, straight-faced.

"Earthquake?" Fasraben repeated, while the Abnorms just looked puzzled.

"Ignore him," Ginny advised. "He was just joking."

Fasraben frowned. He definitely did not like teasing. Nevertheless, he took her advice. He turned his back on Lenny and began detailing his plan to get the buildings down.

"How the... how are we going to get a tree down?" Derrick objected.

Fasraben's plan was to make a battering ram using the trunk of a tree. By ramming the building, they would bring it all down, making climbing into the rubble less dangerous.

Hamid didn't really like the idea; Fasraben had no idea how sturdy concrete buildings were, but since he had nothing else to offer he decided to go along with the basic plan. "We'll need to stay clear of the buildings when we're ramming them, or they will fall on us"

"That is no a problem," Fasraben insisted.

"What are we going to use to cut down the tree?" Lenny was openly derisive. "Our bare hands?"

"Let's find one already down," Angela suggested.

"A tree on the ground may no be strong," Fasraben objected.

"It's easier to get. We could try that first." Hamid had a feeling Fasraben was vetoing the idea only because it was suggested by a girl. Besides, it would take a while to chop down a tree. They only had small axes and no large farming equipment, not even a saw.

Fasraben frowned. "The plan is mine. We should do it the way as I suggested."

There was an uncomfortable silence.

"I'm not knocking your plan," Hamid said evenly. "But Angela suggested an easier way. If that doesn't work, we can always go chop down a tree."

Dystaran unexpectedly came to his rescue. "No all the trees on the ground are weak. It is an idea we could try Fasraben."

Fasraben was not pleased, but he gave a short nod. "Find you a tree," he said abruptly. He remained standing in the exact spot, his hands folded across his chest, as the others hunted a fallen tree.

They got their tree. Finding one really wasn't a problem.

"What a sore loser," Lenny muttered, as he and Hamid bent over their tree.

Hamid nodded, but didn't say anything. Fasraben was definitely going to be a problem.

Gamnic heard Lenny's comment. He grinned. "Do no mind Fasraben. It is that he likes to work. For me to cut down a tree is a work I do no need."

Hamid nodded again. He still felt that Fasraben was going to be a problem. He decided to keep his opinion to himself for now. After all, there was not much he could do.

After trimming away most of the branches, they used the remainder as handles to lift the tree. They now had a battering ram!

Fasraben relented slightly and helped in the ramming of the building, but his general uncooperative attitude continued, especially when his battering ram plan turned out to be basically ineffective.

Following a short debate, they abandoned the battering ram plan and began climbing into one crumbling building after another, after first checking to make sure the building was relatively stable. In a former clothing store, Lenny was able to unearth the necessary scraps of old paper and fabric that he hoped could be used to make paper. The clothing store also provided bundles of fabric in relatively good condition. Good! It would be used to make badly needed clothes. They also packed as much scrap metal as they could carry – metal would always come in handy. They discovered that plastic was virtually indestructible and decided to collect a large quantity of plastic containers in relatively good condition. Then, in a general store they found beautifully preserved ceramic bowls, and other metallic kitchen utensils. They were marveling over these finds when Lenny's shouts brought them to a jewelry store. He had dug a mini crater in the rubble, and peeking through centuries of grime, dust and dirt, was a fortune. A fortune in gold and silver items!

Derrick scooped up a handful of gold jewelry. "I'm rich!" He yelled.

"I'm positive I can get some of these watches to work," Lenny said as he examined some rusty name brand watches.

"Take them," Hamid advised. "Even if they never work, we should be able to make use of the parts."

The villagers were amazed. In Manhattan the rubble that still existed had been stripped clean of any valuables years ago.

"Other communities do no have these," Dystaran said excitedly. He turned to Fasraben. "It is possible we could gather these golds for trade."

Fasraben frowned. "This is something we must think on."

"But if the Trumen find out how valuable the rubbles are, they are likely to kill us to prevent us claiming any of it." Angela was now deeply worried.

Hamid frowned. Angela was right. For years the Trumen had stayed in Manhattan. They thought they had stripped the land of all its valuables centuries ago, so had never seen the need to venture into the Bronx. The Abnorms were in even more danger that they had originally thought.

By nightfall, they were tired, but satisfied that they could carry no more. They returned to camp. Already they were making plans to visit these stores sometime in the near future.

Day one of the return trip went well. They didn't cover as much ground, so were unable to reach the first camping site. On day two they were laden with supplies and heading east when Club started growling. Hamid, who was leading, stopped, forcing the others to halt as well. There was really no place to hide. As usual they were on a lightly wooded road.

"What do we do?" Derrick asked.

"What is it Club? What is it?" Hamid bent to whisper.

Fasraben, from his usual position beside Hamid, murmured. "It is no normal for the animals to attack. No in day. No when we do no attack first.'"

"Tell that to whatever is out there," Lenny muttered as they began backing into each other. They were all carrying huge woven baskets on their backs; and running away would be next to impossible. Besides, they could see nothing. The woods were still and silent.

Club kept up a low continuous growl.

They waited. Nothing happened.

"It is possible a sick animal," Fasraben finally said. "It is no normal for the animals to attack unless they are first attacked. Only the animal sick with the rabies will do strange things."

"We can't stay like this forever," Lenny began.

"Fasraben! Look out!" Hamid screamed. It was a wild dog, and it was leaping straight at Fasraben. Fasraben grabbed out his spear but did not get a chance to defend himself. With a low growl Club leapt at the dog!

The two animals collided in midair then fell to the ground with a thud. The wild dog was no fool. Club was a good thirty pounds heavier. As soon as it was able to get free of Club's surprise attack it turned and dashed off into the woods.

"Oh my God! Oh my God!" Ginny cried in relief.

Hamid started toward Club.

"Do no touch him!" Fasraben shouted as Club looked up with the canine equivalent of surprise.

"What?" Hamid merely looked puzzled.

"He may have got the rabies."

Hamid just stared. Club came panting up to him his tongue hanging out, his tail waving vigorously.

"Keep him away!" Fasraben shouted again. He began backing away, the alarm in his voice sufficient to stop Club. The dog cocked his head as if to say, 'what's up?'

Dystaran began explaining urgently. "When the animals act strange, it is because of the rabies. The disease is very deadly. Club fought the wild dog and may have got scratched, so he now has it. If you touch Club, you too will get it!"

"Sit, Club!" Hamid turned to Fasraben for a clearer explanation and was just in time to see the older boy pull out an arrow.

"What are you doing?" He made an agonized dash toward Fasraben. Too late! Fasraben's arrow left his bow just as Hamid tackled him. As the boys fell, the arrow pierced Club's chest, just between the forelegs.

"No!" Hamid shouted. He scrambled to his feet and started toward Club. The dog had fallen and was now lying deathly still.

Chapter 8

Dystaran grabbed Hamid's T-shirt. "It had to be!" he tried to explain. "It was the only way."

"No! No! No!" Hamid tried to shrug him off. He was concentrating on one thing – reaching Club.

"You can no touch the dog!" Fasraben shouted. "You can no touch the dog! You will die."

In sudden fury, Hamid punched Dystaran in the stomach, momentarily winding him. "Let go! Get the...."

Gamnic unexpectedly joined them, grabbing Hamid from behind. "Listen, Hamid! You can no touch the dog!"

Hamid tried twisting away, but Gamnic held on. Fighting in earnest now, he punched at Gamnic but missed. Dystaran joined the fray again.

"Hey!" Derrick cried out. "Wait a minute. That's two on one!"

Hamid wasn't sure how it happened. Within minutes he, Derrick and Lenny were in a tangle of arms and legs, rolling on the ground and fighting the Abnorms. The girls were screaming and Fasraben was shouting something.

It was sheer exhaustion plus the fear of hurting the girls that finally brought the fighting to a halt. One by one the girls started trying to drag the boys apart. They were getting in the way and to avoid hitting them the boys finally gave up. Hamid looked around.

He was totally exhausted. Dystaran was still holding him from behind. The others stood panting or doubled over, nursing bruised knuckles and other assorted body injuries. Lenny had a nosebleed that Ginny was crying over while both Derrick and Gamnic sported swollen eyes. Lente was crying her eyes out while Angela just stood looking at him, tears streaming down her face.

For a while, the panicked sounds of nature being disturbed were mixed with the girls crying and the boys' heavy, exhausted breathing. Then Hamid made a move to free his arm. Dystaran immediately tightened his grip.

"Hamid I am sorry, but the disease is real." Dystaran panted as Hamid stood still again. He really was too exhausted to struggle further. "If you touched Club, you would be dead in one, maybe two weeks. Fasraben speaks true."

Hamid stared straight ahead and said nothing.

Dystaran tried again. "Hamid..."

"Let me go," Hamid muttered.

"You will no touch the dog?"

Hamid felt like screaming. He shook his head. Once released, he sank to the ground. Some leader he was... but Club was dead! Dead!

He covered his face with his hands and began to cry. He was silent, but his entire body shook with his grief. He couldn't help himself.

"Hamid you would no be able to touch him ever," Dystaran tried yet again to explain.

Hamid did not answer. He remained hunched over, his head buried in his hands.

After a while, since he did not move, Lente bent over him. She and the other girls had stopped crying now and the birds, having recovered from their fright, had resumed singing.

"Leave me! Just leave me!" He cried; his voice

anguished.

Lente stood up. No one else approached him. After a while the others moved some distance away.

It was a few more minutes before Hamid finally lifted his head to stare at Club. Club was lying in a pool of blood. Hamid groaned aloud. He dashed the back of his hand across his face, wiping away the tears. Club was dead! He couldn't believe Club was dead. No! Not Club!

For months he had literally begged his mother for a puppy. He had promised to do everything – clean his room, paint the house, clean up the yard, take out the garbage – anything. Then finally a friend of his mother needed to get rid of a half-breed German Shepherd puppy. His parents were persuaded. He got Club!

Club became Hamid's dog. Even Club recognized that fact. Hamid fed him. Hamid took him on his walks. Hamid played with him. Club only tolerated the other members of Hamid's family. It was Hamid's bed that Club sometimes crawled into at nights.

Hamid doubled over again. He can't be dead! Not Club!

He was so caught up in his grief that it took a while for him to hear Angela speaking.

She was kneeling beside him. Without embarrassment he turned his face into her shoulder. His shoulders shook again. Angela continued speaking softly. "That's how I feel about my parents. It was just them and me. I still cry at nights when I think about them. We were so close... my mother and me." She paused. "And my dad.... We used to take trips together and everything. Ginny doesn't understand 'cause she wasn't close to her parents. But I miss mine awfully. Even though I am not dead, and they are not dead it's just as if they are."

Hamid took some deep breaths. He hugged Angela. After a while, as Angela began sniffing, he wasn't even sure who was comforting who. He wiped his arm across his face again. Then he nodded and struggled to his feet, while keeping his head down. In truth he hadn't thought about his parents much in the last few weeks. He had become so caught up in their lives here. It was overwhelming yet thrilling. There was so much to take care of; so much to do... It was like a strange and compelling adventure. Now he felt ashamed. Angela was right. His parents most likely believed he and Lente were dead. They were all his parents had. They must be devastated. He squeezed his eyes tightly shut. Up until now, he thought he was having fun. It was one big adventure. It was no longer fun! This was real! And now Club was dead!

Angela stood as well. The others had gone, allowing them a degree of privacy. She was now hugging herself. He could feel her eyes watching him, but he refused to look at her.

After staring blankly at Club for a while, Hamid finally moved. "I guess I'll have to bury him."

They slowly moved to join the others. Angela pointed to a spot just beyond a rise. "Look! It looks like they're digging a grave."

Hamid nodded, and turned. "I'll bring Club."

"Remember you can't touch him," Angela reminded anxiously.

He just walked off. Yes, he knew he was being uncaring and selfish to walk away from Angela like that but he was now embarrassed – he had cried all over her! Besides, he couldn't face her or any other form of comfort right now. He was afraid he would start crying again.

What he really wanted to do was to curl up in a ball somewhere – by himself.

As soon as he started toward Club the others wandered back. They obviously didn't trust him and perhaps thought he would touch the dog. Hamid ignored them and did not respond even when Gamnic give him a piece of deer skin, after telling him that he could use it to wrap Club's body. Taking extra care not to touch Club, he used sticks to roll the body onto the deer skin. His facial expression didn't encourage help, and no one offered as he dragged Club's body over to the makeshift grave. After filling in the grave Hamid covered it with as many rocks as he could. No way did he want Club's body eaten by wild animals.

Afterwards, there were mummers of, "Sorry Hamid..." as the others again moved away and gave him some privacy.

Hamid knelt beside the grave.

"I'm sorry Club..." he paused and blinked. He would *not* start crying again. He took some deep breaths. "'Bye Club. I'll really miss you."

Standing, he dusted off his hands and turned to join the others. They did not travel far before deciding to make camp for the night. At first Hamid just stood, then he sat staring at the ground, listening without contributing anything. Now and again, he felt their stares, but nobody said anything directly to him. No one, until Fasraben spoke.

"You give me the maps and compass. If so I can lead tomorrow."

Hamid's head jerked up. He couldn't believe... The nerve of this guy!

"No!" He forcefully rejected the idea. For once, he

didn't care how rude he sounded. He had never liked Fasraben, but now he actively disliked him. And it didn't matter how many times he told himself that Fasraben may well have saved his life – Club could not have been allowed to live. Fact was fact – Club had saved Fasraben, yet Club was dead and Fasraben had killed him. And that fact kept clouding any and all feelings he had for Fasraben.

Fasraben started to say something but stopped. He finally shrugged his shoulders. "It is that I wish to help you. Tomorrow you may no feel to lead."

Hamid turned his back on him and rolled out his blanket. "I'll take last watch. Wake me." With that he closed his eyes and pretended to sleep.

His actions effectively dampened the mood of the camp. One by one the others settled down to sleep.

*****

Angela woke him. Hamid struggled up from a deep disturbing dream. He was running in the woods, trying to escape a pack of wild dogs....

"Wha..?"

"Lenny woke me," she said. "It's your watch."

Hamid sat up. Lenny was already sleeping or pretending to sleep.

"Just now?" he asked. "He just now woke you?"

"Well...." Angela gave him a guilty look.

Hamid rubbed his eyes. "You should have waked me up," he muttered. "And why did he wake you anyway? You were not supposed to be on guard."

Angela shrugged.

Hamid remained silent as he sat and hugged his knees, aware that Angela was watching him. He finally gave a deep sigh. "Thanks. For today.... I mean yesterday. I didn't mean to be rude to you."

She moved closer – cautiously.

Hamid gave her a rueful grin. Angela gave him a relieved smile. Within minutes, they were within touching distance. With heads bent, they began whispering quietly so as not to disturb the others. Mostly they talked about the past and their hopes and dreams for the future before this strange adventure began.

*****

The next day Hamid took the lead. He tried to pretend that nothing unusual had happened. It was hard. Every now and again he would automatically reach for Club, to pat him or to touch him, only to be painfully reminded of his loss. His one cheerful accomplishment was Fasraben – or the lack of him. Fasraben was finally leaving him alone. The Truman had taken two more insults before deciding that it just wasn't worth it to walk beside Hamid.

Without Fasraben to annoy him, and with Angela by his side, Hamid bad mood visibly improved. By early evening, as they walked into the Village, he was even chatting with Lenny and Derrick again.

*****

Three weeks later, they were again planning another trip. Hamid, Lenny and Derrick had spent the weeks building a log cabin for themselves. They were tired of sleeping with the little boys. Their cabin was rectangular shaped but had three separate rooms and separate entrances – really three cabins in one. Lenny had insisted he needed privacy. Neither Hamid nor Derrick questioned his insistence; they knew he and Ginny were close. After a lot of pleading from the girls, they also built a single cabin that the three girls could share.

During that time Hamid had reached a simple solution to what he secretly called his 'hostilities with Fasraben' – he totally avoided the Truman. Although he spoke to Dystaran and Gamnic, he used the excuse of helping Lenny sort supplies collected from Fordham Road to avoided Treber. After all, Fasraben was Treber's son. He felt guilty being rude to Fasraben. Now with another trip in the works there would be no avoiding Fasraben. Technically, Fasraben would be the leader of the upcoming trip although Hamid was supposed to be the guide. So now they would be forced into each other's company. Hamid even wondered if Treber wasn't deliberately trying to get them together. It was Treber who suggested the trip.

Every three months the Abnorms met the Trumen from Manhattan at a prearranged pick-up point. It was there the Trumen would leave their Abnorm children. This time around the Abnorms decided to scout the spot a week in advance. They were worried that the Trumen may have set an ambush for them, and the last thing they needed was to walk into it. Originally, the Abnorms had escaped Manhattan by boat. From the shoreline they had found their way to the train tracks. These were the tracks they had followed north.

So now the group, there were six of them in all – the girls had been persuaded to stay behind – were following the Number Two train line, heading south. It took close to four days. They arrived at the spot late evening when the sun was just going down. Instead of going directly to the meeting spot, they left the tracks and climbed to higher ground to scout the area.

"What do you think?" Lenny asked as they all crouched low on the sparsely wooded hillside near what used to be a road.

"No one is near," Fasraben said.

Hamid was not so sure. "I don't like it." As he looked around, he tried to figure out what it was he didn't like. Certainly, there was no lack of sound to make him cautious. He was now accustomed to the constant racket of birds and small insects or animals in the trees. Here, was no different. Maybe the problem was that the area was just too open. Where they stood, he had a clear view of the small clearing that served as the meeting spot. The trouble was, so too did anyone on the surrounding hills.

"I do no see a problem," Fasraben insisted.

Hamid ignored him. He waved towards the woods as he turned to Dystaran. "An army could hide in those hills. Let's circle back. You did say that when you came over to the Bronx you came by boat. Where are the boats?"

"Those we hid," Dystaran said.

"Could you take us to the hiding place?" Hamid asked.

"Planning something?" Lenny asked with a knowing look.

"We need to warn Dystaran's father that this spot may have been discovered."

"That is if they did no already kill him," Dystaran muttered.

"That was no a part of the plan," Fasraben inserted. "We come only to check this spot. We did no come to warn anyone."

For the first time in weeks Hamid looked directly at Fasraben. "We need to warn them," he insisted. "They will walk into a trap otherwise."

"This is no a fact," Fasraben said.

Hamid started to his feet. "You can always camp here until we come back."

Fasraben stood also. "I will come with you. However, I have given my warning. This is a trip you will regret."

*****

The boats were missing from their hiding spot. Was that a bad omen? Hamid wondered.

"What do we now?" Dystaran asked.

There had to be another way. Frowning, Hamid looked around as he searched for an inspiration.

"I've got it!" he grinned. "Do you remember that the train to Manhattan went under the river?"

"You think...." Derrick's voice trailed off.

Lenny frowned, "But is it still there?"

"There is only one way to find out." Hamid turned. "Let's go back to the train tracks."

"I do no understand." Fasraben and the other villagers looked confused.

Hamid quickly explained that long ago trains traveled from the Bronx to Manhattan through an underground tunnel.

"So, if that tunnel is still there we can use it," Lenny finished.

Finding the tunnel was not easy. They had to hike through the dense thick forest and undergrowth and down some steep slopes where the tracks disappeared into the earth. After members of the group twice tripped on broken metallic pieces of the old train tracks, Hamid decided it was safer to avoid the tracks altogether. He didn't need injuries. And falling on a piece of projected metal bar would be no fun. They walked parallel to the tracks. Using the long knives that the Abnorms used when farming, they hacked their way down, carving a narrow path. It took the better part of two hours before Derrick's shout stopped them.

"This is it!" He had stumbled into a dark tunnel.

They crowded around. Yes, it was the tunnel. Because of the lack of light, there was little plant growth. Even so, mud had piled up over the years and the tracks were no longer visible.

"Is it safe?" Gamnic was doubtful.

"There is no water coming out so the roof must be intact." Hamid said.

"Yeah," Lenny agreed. "I think it should be okay. Remember we used to hear about water mains under Manhattan that were over one hundred years old."

"Sure," Derrick muttered. "We used to hear about them breaking and flooding people's homes too."

"Hamid!" Lenny suddenly called out. Hamid turned.

"If we get transported back home without the girls, I'll murder you." Lenny *was* serious.

Chapter 9

Hamid looked into the inky blackness of the tunnel and hesitated. That, he hadn't thought of. Would he be able to face his parents if he ever got back and Lente did not?

"Why would this tunnel take you back?" Dystaran was curious.

"We don't know what it will do," Lenny said. "We didn't expect the first one to take us forward in time, yet it did."

Gamnic stared at them. Hamid gave him a quick look. He had forgotten that Gamnic did not know where they were from. Well, it was too late to hide the facts now. With a shrug he explained. Seeing Gamnic's unbelieving look, Dystaran backed up Hamid's tale. Even so the Abnorm did not really seem to believe them. Gamnic's disbelief lasted until Hamid pulled out a flashlight and switched it on before starting forward.

"What tool is that?" Dystaran grinned at Gamnic's amazed exclamation and eagerly explained. Fasraben had not seen the flashlight before and was equally intrigued.

With the explanations over, Hamid again turned his concentration to the tunnel. As the guide, there was no way he could send the others and not go through the tunnel himself. He could not abandon his responsibilities, but he didn't have to involve everyone. "Lenny, you and

Derrick could wait for us here."

"No way!" Lenny said adamant.

"Same here!" Derrick agreed. "If you go, I go."

"But...."

Lenny scowled and for a moment looked hesitant. "You had better say some deep prayers. We're not staying," he said with finality.

In the end, they all went. Mud slides and possible flooding over the years had reduced the original height of the tunnel considerably. They could still walk upright, but in some areas it was close. The mud in the tunnel was a damp slushy mess. In one area they were ankle deep in the slush.

"I just hope there are no snakes in this stuff," Lenny muttered as he cautiously lifted his foot. His movement was accompanied by a loud sucking sound which was constantly repeated as the others went through the same motions.

There were a few good areas where the ground was firm and dry. Then they would try in vain to remove as much of the mud as they could from their boots, legs and clothing. After traveling for a while, they were forced to stop. The wide tunnel was now a narrow passage.

"The wall came down." Lenny stated the obvious as he shone his light up and down the rubble of mud and concrete.

Hamid stared at the narrow passage. "It's wide enough. We should be able to get through."

"Yeah," Derrick agreed. "But should we? I mean, what's on the other side?"

After another close look, Hamid made up his mind. "There is only one way to find out." He started forward. "Wait here," he called to them. "Let me just check first."

He slowly inched his way around the rubble. The passage had narrowed to slightly less than three feet wide. Hamid cautiously examined the crumbling walls. His flashlight revealed that although the debris was loose it didn't look as if it was going anywhere. He continued. The narrowed passage went on for a distance of close to twenty feet, then the area widened again. Hamid breathed a sigh of relief.

"It's safe," he called. "The walls are okay on this side. You can all come."

It didn't take them long. Following Hamid's lead, they squeezed pass the rubble and continued the journey.

"What's this?" Derrick called as his light picked up a high ledge.

"I think this area was a station and that is the passengers' platform," Lenny said as he too looked at the ledge.

That was not good enough for Fasraben. Once again, they had to give a detailed explanation before they could move on, but at least the rest of the journey went without incident. It took a little over an hour to get to the other side. The exit there was even narrower than on the Bronx side, because of a rockslide close to the opening. They dug their way out. They were now in Trumen's land – safe for now because of the thick woods.

"I am better able to know this place." Fasraben said as they stepped out of the tunnel. "I will lead."

Hamid decided not to challenge his knowledge. It was now dark and besides, Fasraben had been surprisingly cooperative up to this point. He nodded.

At first the scenery was just the same. After hacking their way out of the thick woods, they came to the lightly wooded streets and crumbling buildings. Slowly however, the view changed. The Trumen had settled mainly in the upper sections of Manhattan, on either side of Central Park. Here the streets were really streets, mostly paved with red bricks. The homes too, were made of brick, some as high as four stories. It was obvious that over the years, unsafe apartments and buildings had been knocked down leaving open spaces or sometimes piles of rubble. In some areas unusual curves in the road indicated that the houses were built on the former streets and a new road carved through the rubble of the former homes.

As they walked, they tried staying as close as possible to the buildings. Although it was dark, the moon was out and no one wanted to attract attention. Two tense-filled hours later, Dystaran was slipping open the latch of his parent's house.

"All wait here," he instructed. "I will check upstairs."

Hamid looked around. They were in the living room. The floor was covered with a lovely, quilted rug so they crowded the door, not wanting to soil the rug with muddy boots. There were two sofas, one big and one small, all arranged around a huge fireplace. Of course there was no television or radio just a big bookcase filled with a number of bounded books. Hamid slipped off his boots and walked over to them; Lenny and Derrick followed. They did not recognize any of the titles. Hamid turned as Dystaran returned with his parents.

Looking at them Hamid would have said they were about seventy. Dystaran's mother's hair was all white and she had the deep blue eyes and dark skin of her brother, Treber. His father was stooping and used a cane. His salt and pepper hair was cut short, and although his features and complexion were white his hair was definitely that of a black person. It was from him Dystaran had got his brown eyes. Both Trumen were dressed in long flowing robes. Hamid was not sure if the robes were night clothing or regular day wear. They looked very similar to the robes worn by the villagers.

Dystaran's parents were eager to hear news of the Village. In turn, they explained that because of the carelessness of a fellow Truman the Supreme Liberty had come to know about the meeting point.

"They do no suspect me," his father explained. "Fortunately, the Truman who was named as the suspect is already dead."

Fasraben nodded. "They deliberately gave the name of a dead man."

Both Dystaran's parents smiled.

"Hamid has another plan, father," Dystaran now said.

As they walked through the tunnel Hamid had come up with his plan and now he explained it to Dystaran's family. The new meeting spot would never be the same from month to month. At each meeting, a map would be left giving directions on where to leave the next group of Abnorm children. Hamid also insisted that only Dystaran's family should know of the tunnel. Parents leaving their children would have to come to the Bronx by boat as they did before. They also set a day – a month from now – for the next pickup.

"It will no be a problem." Dystaran's brother liked the new plan. Dystaran had woken both him and a sister and quickly made the introductions.

"Can you also get us guns and ammunition?" Hamid asked. "You could leave them in the tunnel. Just make sure no one follows you." With the help of Dystaran and Fasraben, he drew a rough diagram.

"What?" Dystaran's father sounded shocked.

Hamid just stared at him. "You know they plan to attack us soon. We will have to defend ourselves."

The older man sighed, and then looked away. "I know. I know. I have tried, but members of the Supreme Liberty will no listen. The rule of Scigam left them much afraid. Abnorms will live much longer than us. There is much fear that if the village of Abnorms is allowed to grow, soon the Abnorms there will kill us Trumen."

"We only want that they leave us alone," Dystaran cried.

His father sighed again. "They will no do that." He shook his head sadly. "I will bring you the guns... but please you will be careful. If it is possible do no fight. Remember, one day you may be fighting your brother."

The brothers exchanged looks. Hamid still found it hard to believe they were brothers. Dystaran's brother looked about forty and Dystaran was actually the oldest child of his parents!

"We would never kill each other," Dystaran vowed.

Although his brother agreed, their father was still unhappy.

They didn't stay much longer after that. It was a little after twelve o'clock and the last thing they needed was to get caught in Trumen's land in the daytime.

*****

"We need horses," Lenny said suddenly. They had just left Dystaran's former home and were passing a small stable.

"What is it you mean?" Fasraben frowned.

"Horses – animals that have four legs – they are likely sleeping in that barn-like structure over there." He pointed in the direction of the stable.

This time, Fasraben actually scowled. Lenny grinned. That was the most emotion Lenny had got out of him yet. Hamid hurriedly interrupted.

"Lenny is right. If we could get horses to the village, we would be able to get around much better."

"You would steal a horse?"

Hamid hastily smothered his smile. It was difficult! The scowl was increasing. Even Dystaran and Gamnic were staring.

"I wouldn't call it stealing exactly," Lenny said casually. "This is a war. They are trying to kill us. We need to defend ourselves the best way we can. I call it building our defenses."

Fasraben was still frowning. Gamnic gave him a cautious glance before explaining. "This is no a good place to take the horses. These horses are ordinary travelers' horses. They are gelded and no be used for breeding. The good horses are at Nesnor's horse farm. Nesnor is a horse breeder, but to get there we would need to go west."

"How far," Lenny asked.

"Half of an hour maybe more."

Hamid took a quick look at his watch. "We have five hours to daylight. Do you think we can make it?"

Gamnic hesitated, and then nodded. "The time is no long so we could."

"Let's go then," Hamid said.

"I will come, but I do no agree with this plan," Fasraben stated abruptly.

"Don't injure your conscience," Lenny said flippantly. "Stay."

Fasraben ignored him.

*****

They were at the farm in less than twenty minutes.

"Are you sure there are no guards?" Derrick asked for the fifth time.

"No." Gamnic had worked at the farm as a child. He now patiently explained again. "What is the need for guards? All know Nesnor's horses. It would be foolish to steal one. All the boys come and work in the days and go home at the nights. No one sleeps here with the horses."

They crouched below a low fence and surveyed the stables. The stables were a good distance from the main house, and they were really two barn-like wooden buildings, joined by a flat roofed corridor. The group was standing, behind the last of six fenced training areas; they were still some distance from the stable.

"The best horses are kept in that one." Gamnic pointed to the larger barn structure.

"Let's not push our luck," Lenny muttered. "We can get horses from the other one."

"Are you sure?" Derrick was still being unusually cautious.

Hamid turned to him in query. "What's up?"

Derrick shrugged, "I don't know. I just feel we've been too lucky so far."

"Well, we're here now," Lenny said. "Are we going to do it or what?"

Hamid looked at Fasraben, but Fasraben had resumed his usual expressionless face. Dystaran seemed excited and so too Gamnic.

"Let's go," he said.

They silently climbed over each fence until they were able to enter the stable. Once inside, they closed the doors then Hamid, Lenny and Derrick turned on their flashlights.

"It is best if everyone waits here," Gamnic instructed. "I will bring the horses to you."

"Here, take my light," Hamid said.

Gamnic found a barrel of apples and told them to take some. Then he walked up the aisles. One or two of the horses nickered. Gamnic began murmuring in a low soothing voice as he examined one horse after another. Finally, he brought out the first horse. It was a beautiful mare.

"We need at least one stallion," Dystaran said as he quickly began saddling and bridling the mare.

Gamnic hesitated. "The stallions are no kept here with the mares. They are in the other barn."

"Let's not push our luck," Hamid muttered. "We can take a stallion some other time."

Lenny suddenly remembered a critical bit of information. "We can't ride."

It was the villagers' turn to stare.

"You no can ride a horse?" Dystaran asked. His astonishment was clear in his voice.

"Remember, where we come from...." Derrick began.

Hamid interrupted, "We don't need to ride. We can lead the horses. Look, let's hurry. We'll sort that out after we leave with the horses."

Gamnic turned just as the doors to the stable opened again.

Derrick and Lenny quickly switched off their lights. Gamnic was not swift enough. He was still fumbling with the switch when a new voice called.

"What goes on? Gamnic! What do you here?"

The Truman had not yet seen the others. He stood by the door, holding a lighted torch. Gamnic stood frozen as the man approached.

"What do you here?" The Truman repeated more amazed than anything else.

Slowly, stealthily Fasraben began creeping up behind the Truman. His plan, if the plan was to disable the Truman, almost worked. At the last minute, some sixth sense must have warned the Truman. He turned.

Fasraben immediately launched himself at the man. They both fell to the floor. The torch went flying. Fasraben scrambled quickly to his feet, but the man came at him swinging a viscous fist. He connected squarely with Fasraben's jaw and the younger Truman staggered.

"Fire! Fire!" Gamnic shouted. The torch had landed in the hay! The stables were on fire!

"The horses! Save the horses!" The Truman abandoned the fight without hesitation. He began running toward the stalls. "We can no put out the fire. Save the horses!"

After a moment of hesitation, they all ran toward the stalls to help lead out the horses. The Truman was momentarily confused when he realized he had so much help, but within minutes he had them organized. He began issuing swift instructions as the flames spread rapidly.

Someone, most likely the Truman, began ringing a bell.

"Oh, shoot! We have to get out of here!" Hamid said in between coughs. He had made three trips so far into the stable to bring out one horse at a time. He turned to Dystaran who was at his side. "Where are the others? We've got to go. More people will come now that he rang that bell."

Dystaran coughed, "I do no know. I saw Gamnic, but...." He looked around. The entire area was now well lit with light from the burning barns. Flames were already shooting out of the barn's roof. From the direction of the main house, there came a shout. More Trumen!

"If you see any of the others tell them to each get a horse – any horse – and go to the last fence. Go now! Quickly! And don't go back into the barns. Circle around them."

Hamid did not follow his own advice. He raced back to the barn. It was impossible to go in again. He raised his arm to protect his face. Even a yard from the entrance the heat of the fire was intense. "Lenny! Derrick! Gamnic!" he shouted.

"Is it that someone is inside?" It was another Truman, and for now the man did not realize that Hamid was not Truman.

"I do no know. I can no find them." Hamid tried to mimic the speech patterns of the Trumen, but also kept his arm over his face and pretended to cough, hoping to disguise his accent.

"Where went Yorlink?"

Hamid had no idea who Yorlink was. "He was helping...." He waved his free arm vaguely in the direction of the second barn. "I do no know...." He was coughing again, bending almost double in the process.

The man rushed off. The fire had swept across the roof to the second barn. However, unlike the first barn, that barn was not totally engulfed in flames.

Hamid circled the barns twice, shouting as he went. He found none of the others. His only hope was that they were already gone with Dystaran. Finally, he made his way to the fence, leading a horse.

Dystaran, Gamnic, and Derrick were already there. Gamnic led three horses, Dystaran and Derrick one each. There was no sign of Lenny, or Fasraben.

"I was able to get a stallion," Gamnic said. He pointed

to the horse Dystaran led.

"But we can't stay here with these horses," Derrick warned.

"Keep down," Hamid hissed as Derrick stood up. "They will think the horses are by themselves and still fenced in if they can't see us. Besides, everybody is too busy fighting the fire." He paused and looked around. "Anybody saw Lenny, or Fasraben?"

"No recently," Dystaran said.

Derrick gave him a worried look. "I just knew we shouldn't have come."

"What do we do now?" Gamnic asked.

"Soon it is day light," Dystaran warned.

Hamid looked at his watch. They had spent over one hour fighting the fire. They couldn't stay here much longer, but where were the other two?

"I hope they weren't stupid enough to get trapped in the barn," Derrick muttered.

Hamid turned to stare at the burning buildings. If they had, they were dead.

"Half-hour. We'll give them another half-hour. Then we have to leave."

Dystaran objected, "But..."

"If daylight catches us in this town, we are *all* dead." Hamid interrupted. "We definitely can't stay." Although he sounded firm, inside he felt a knot slowly tightening in his chest. How would he face Ginny if he didn't bring Lenny back? And much as he disliked Fasraben he certainly didn't wish him dead.

They settled down, sitting on the ground to wait. There was silence since no one felt in the mood to talk.

Half an hour passed. Hamid looked at his watch. "Twenty more minutes."

Twenty minutes came and went. No one moved.

Hamid finally shifted. For a moment he stared at the gathering crowd of Trumen. They had started a bucket brigade to pour water and the fire and had finally brought it under control. "We have to go. Can you lead Dystaran?"

Dystaran nodded. Silently, the group started making their way back to the tunnel, leading the stallion and the four mares. Hamid kept looking back, hoping to see the others and checking to see if they were being followed. However, no one started in their direction; the crowd was still focused on the barns. And there was still no sign of their missing friends.

They reached the tunnel just before daylight.

"We *can't* just leave them," Derrick said as he ran his hand nervously across the back of his neck.

"I've thought about it," Hamid said quietly. "We will go to the other side and try to find food and so on. Tonight we'll come back. Dystaran, we can check your parents again and see if they heard anything."

Dystaran nodded. At least they had a plan. He and Gamnic turned to the task of getting the horses into the tunnel. It was not easy. The animals were clearly frightened and balked at the dark entrance. It took minutes of patience plus apples and brute force to get them moving. Once started however, the stallion led his mares, and they were able to maintain a steady pace.

"I hope..." Derrick stopped, unwilling to voice his fears aloud.

"Me too," Hamid murmured. He hoped they were alive, although he didn't see how they could be. He wearily rubbed his temples. He had the beginnings of a massive tension headache. What could have happened?

Could they have been trapped in the barn? If the Trumen had found them there would have be a lot more shouting and carrying on. He was sure they hadn't been found. So where were they? Lenny would take a few chances, but Fasraben wasn't the type to do anything even remotely risky – unless he went in to rescue Lenny. That still left the question, 'Where were they?'

*****

While Hamid and Dystaran slept, the others spent the next day foraging for food on the Bronx side of the tunnel. Since they had to stay near the tunnel, they also spent some time camouflaging the entrance and the passage leading up to it. They hobbled the horses, and left them to graze at the camp, which was some distance away. Later that night, Hamid and Dystaran got up, ate, and then made their way back to the tunnel. The others would remain at the camp.

Some hours later, Dystaran quietly made his way into his house.

As soon as he opened the door a voice called. "Dystaran?"

"Yes?"

It was his brother. Dystaran and Hamid quickly slipped inside.

"Come," the Truman said. "This way. They only now got here."

"They are here?" Hamid had been afraid to hope. "Thank God!" It was a barely audible mutter as he came further into the room "What happened?"

Fasraben replied. "Lenny was injured by a beam of the barn. He was no able to move. It took I and Yorlink to rescue him. After, we could no escape the fire. We hid in a place under the barn's floor that Yorlink showed us. No one found us. It was stuffy, but the fire did no trouble us. Last night and in the day it was no possible to come out. There were too many people. It was only tonight that we felt it is safe to come out."

"Who is Yorlink?" Hamid asked absently. He was looking at the still form of Lenny. His friend had not moved.

"The groom," Dystaran explained. "The man Fasraben fought."

"Is he okay?" Hamid asked, nodding in Lenny's direction. Lenny looked dead to him. He was lying on the bed, his eyes closed, and his arms by his side. He had not moved while Hamid watched.

Dystaran's father, who had also entered, shrugged. "With rest he should be. It is that his legs were burned by the fire. Also, it is that he has a bad bruise to his right leg. I have wrapped it. He is no able to walk now, but he should heal. I have given him the drink of the Weet tree. It will make him sleep a lot, but he will feel no pain."

Hamid moved a little closer to the bed. Oh! Sleeping, he thought with relief. He turned to Fasraben. "This Yorlink – will he be a problem?"

"No. He wishes to come with us."

"Why?"

"My daughter was Abnorm; she was killed two years ago at the time of the wipe-out." Hamid was startled as Yorlink himself replied. The man had quietly entered the room.

Yorlink continued, "My wife is long dead. The son of my son was also Abnorm. He was only three when they took him. We have no seen him since."

"Why did they no try to save him?" Dystaran

questioned.

"My son is convinced it is for the good of Manhattan that no Abnorm live. The wife of my son killed herself after they took away her only child." He shrugged. "I have no one here. My son is no longer my son."

"Can Lenny travel?" Hamid asked abruptly. He didn't know whether he should believe Yorlink, but now was not the time to argue. They really didn't have much time. "How did you get him here?"

"We rode." Yorlink gave a quick smile. "When we left, we took four horses. I held Lenny before me on the saddle."

Hamid looked around as if expecting to see the horses.

"The horses we put in the stable behind the house," Fasraben said. "They will be easy to retrieve."

After a quick discussion they decided to ride to the tunnel. It would be quicker. Yorlink had taken a stallion and three mares. He would ride the stallion and hold Lenny as before.

"I can't ride," Hamid warned. He was given a fifteen minute crash course in riding. And then they were off!

"It is my hope that they believe the animals you took died in the fire," Yorlink said as they negotiated the streets. "And so far the people at the Nesnor farm seem to believe that I died in the burning barn."

"Still, it is best that we hurry," Dystaran urged. "They will no find your body or the bodies of the horses in the barn and all here will know these horses were stolen." The clip clopping of the horses' hoofs on the cobbled streets were the only sounds, but because of the stillness of the night even those sounds seemed unnaturally loud. "We perhaps should have covered the feet of the horses."

The Intruders. In This War They Had The Advantage

Hamid was clinging to his horse's reins for dear life. He couldn't deal with a reply.

Fasraben, who was in the lead, hissed, "Quiet!"

They continued. As they rounded another block, there was a shouted call.

"Halt!"

Chapter 10

Fasraben stopped, forcing the group to do likewise. Hamid's mare nickered and stepped nervously as he tried to control her. Dystaran came up beside him and grabbed the mare's bridle.

"Who is he?" Hamid whispered as he and Dystaran carefully kept their heads bent.

"Maybe a guard."

The Truman slowly approached. "What do you here at this hour?"

"My friend is sick." Fasraben pointed to Lenny. "It is my wish to take him to the house of my sister. Her husband has much knowledge of healing."

"Then you must hurry." The Truman waved them through the intersection.

Hamid gave a relieved sigh. "That was too close. How is Lenny doing?"

Yorlink looked down. "Still sleeping. If he should awake, I will give him more of the Weet drink."

Hamid nodded and turned his concentration back to controlling the mare he was riding.

They left the town without further incident, but it took another full hour to reach the tunnel. That was just the beginning of their problems. They found that it was hard to ride horses in these woods. A path that was sufficient for the horse was not necessarily good for a horse carrying someone on its back. Branches and leaves kept smacking against their faces; in fact, after going for less than fifteen minutes, Hamid decided that he had had enough.

"Listen, I'm getting down. I would rather walk. My face feels like someone took a belt to it."

There wasn't much disagreement. The only problem was Lenny.

"We can strap him over the horse," Yorlink suggested.

Hamid nodded. "Good idea."

They covered Lenny with a blanket and laid him face down over the stallion. Yorlink led that horse, and the others led their own. At the tunnel they had the same difficulty convincing the horses to enter as before. Fortunately, just as before, once inside the horses gave no trouble.

The sky was just lightening when the weary group trekked into camp.

"Shirts! You found them! You found them!" Derrick cried.

The others were just as noisy with their greetings.

Hamid could only stand with a silly grin on his face as his back was thumped about a dozen times by his friends.

"Thank Fasraben," he kept saying. "Thank Fasraben."

"What's wrong with Lenny?"

"Who is he?"

"What happened to your face?"

"Did someone beat you?"

"Lenny got burned, but he will be okay. This is Yorlink. And nobody whipped me. The tree branches did this to my face." Hamid had to shout to be heard because although there were questions everyone was asking all at once.

While Derrick and Yorlink got Lenny down and settled him comfortably on a blanket on the ground,

Dystaran and Fasraben told the story.

Hamid sat, propped up against a tree and watched and listened. He was tired. His bones left like jelly, yet he didn't feel sleepy. As his gaze kept flickering between Fasraben and Yorlink he tried to sort out his thoughts. They had saved Lenny's life. Yet he wasn't sure he could trust Yorlink... and Fasraben? Hamid leaned back and closed his eyes. He could picture Club in his mind. Club! Shoot! He missed his dog. I have to stop blaming Fasraben, he thought. Maybe Fasraben would never be his best friend, but he was beginning to realize that the Truman did care – in his own way he cared, or he would never have risked his life to rescue Lenny. He opened his eyes as he heard footsteps approaching. Dystaran had come over.

"Why do you no get some sleep?" Dystaran asked. "Or you can eat. We have food. You can eat first if you are hungry."

Hamid looked around. Yorlink and Fasraben were eating. Derrick and Gamnic were not in sight. Actually he just wanted to stay here and do nothing, but he guessed he would have to get up. Besides, he hadn't thanked Fasraben properly.

He struggled to his feet. "Where did Derrick and Gamnic go?"

"They go to put the horses that you brought with the others," Dystaran replied. "Will you come to eat?"

Hamid shook his head. "No. Later maybe. I'll just go over and talk to Fasraben."

Fasraben was still eating. Hamid squatted beside the older boy.

"How is Lenny?" he asked.

Yorlink replied. "I gave to him more of the Weet. He still sleeps. It is better that he sleeps."

Hamid nodded. "Thanks for rescuing him," he said quietly. He then turned to look directly at Fasraben. "Thanks, Fasraben."

Fasraben looked uncomfortable. "I could no leave him there."

Hamid gave him a quick grin. "You could, but I'm thankful that you didn't."

Fasraben was definitely uncomfortable receiving praise. He cleared his throat noisily then changed the subject. "What do we now?"

Hamid gave a genuine smile as he recognized the compliment Fasraben had just paid by asking him. "Rest, for maybe two hours then we head back to the village. We should be able to ride the horses on the old roads."

"Well, we will see very good what will hit us now that it is day," Dystaran grinned.

"My face still hasn't recovered," Hamid said. Tentatively, he touched the welts on his face – areas where branches had whipped at him during their night ride. Dystaran, Fasraben and Yorlink had similar marks on their faces.

"It does look that someone whipped us," Dystaran commented.

"It feels like that too," Hamid said with feeling. He looked over at Fasraben and grinned, inviting the Truman to join his self-mockery. To his surprise Fasraben grinned in return.

They were all still grinning, foolishly at each other, when Derrick and Gamnic returned. Once again the plan was explained. Then Hamid went back to his rest spot while the others packed up in preparation for leaving.

Within two hours they were on their way. Lenny was still asleep and Yorlink rode double with him on the stallion. Their biggest problem was keeping the two stallions apart.

"Are you sure it is okay to keep giving him that drink?" Hamid asked as he took the lead. Yorlink was giving Lenny a few more drops of the Weet.

"He will need it to make the journey," Yorlink said. "I think I will no give him any more for the rest of today. Then he will be awake tonight." After a paused he warned. "If his pain is great, it may be necessary to give him a little."

"How much of the stuff do you have?" Derrick asked.

"Dystaran's father gave me much. Enough for four maybe five days."

Derrick looked at Hamid. Hamid shrugged. It had taken them about almost four days to get here, but with the horses they should be able to half the journey. He just wanted to get home – home meaning the Village. He was afraid for Lenny. And the incident with the fire had worn him out. He was tired of making decisions – tired of being afraid, just plain tired. He wanted to get back as quickly as possible. Then maybe Angela or Sergin, the village healer, could look after Lenny.

Shortly after leaving the camp, Fasraben moved up beside him. Hamid knew things were back to normal when Fasraben began his questions. As he answered, Hamid gave the Truman a rueful look. Just for a minute he briefly regretted thanking Fasraben for saving Lenny. No. He was thankful. He just needed something else to shut Fasraben up!

They made good time completing about a third of the journey before nightfall. Lenny was just waking up and moaning as they stopped to make camp.

With Fasraben's help, Hamid eased him down from

Yorlink's horse. "Take it easy, Lenny. We're getting you down."

"My leg... my leg," Lenny muttered.

They gently lowered him to the ground. Lenny's eyes were still closed, but he continued muttering. Hamid guessed that he was semiconscious. He looked helplessly at Fasraben.

"He should be fine. We should feed him with the soup, then give him more of the Weet."

"What about his leg?" Hamid asked.

Fasraben checked Lenny's legs. It was horribly swollen. "It may be good, but I do no know."

"Best we just wrap it again until we get to your village," Yorlink suggested as he too examined Lenny's legs.

Hamid took a deep breath and nodded. Two more days! It should take them two more days. He just hoped Lenny survived.

*****

As Hamid had predicted, it took two more days to get to the Village. They arrived mid-evening, thankfully without further incident. And Lenny survived. Throughout the journey he had been in so much pain that they kept him drugged with Weet. His legs were still swollen and looked awful. Without antibiotics, Hamid was afraid they would get infected. He didn't know much about medicine and neither did any of the others, so they basically just left the dressings alone and hoped for the best.

A crowd of excited villagers met then. They were marveling over the horses until Ginny and the girls came up.

"Oh my God! What's wrong with Lenny?" Ginny screamed.

Hamid was helping get Lenny down from the horse. "He got burned on his legs. Let's get him to Sergin."

Hamid was not surprised when Ginny began crying. "Is he going to die?"

"Calm down Ginny," he said. "Now that we are here, he should be okay."

"What happened? What happened?"

Everyone wanted to know. Hamid and Yorlink left the others to tell the tale. With Ginny and Angela tagging along, they carried Lenny to Sergin's hut.

Sergin bent over Lenny. He carefully removed the bandages. Ginny took one look at Lenny's legs and began wailing again.

Sergin turned to give her a stern look. "No noise. I can no work in noise."

Ginny turned to bury her face in Hamid's shoulder. He awkwardly patted her, "How does it look?" he asked Sergin.

Sergin was muttering over Lenny's legs. He did not immediately respond. Finally, he looked up, "Angela, bring to me the pouch of herbs," he pointed. "And hot water. We need much of the hot water."

Angela hurried to obey, and then stopped and turned to them, "Maybe you should all come back later. Sergin will take care of him and right now you'll just be in the way."

"Are you sure?" Hamid asked.

"Positive," Angela smiled.

Hamid took a last look at Lenny then turned, "Come Ginny."

She did not want to leave. "But..."

"You heard Angela," Hamid persuaded. The door of the hut opened and Lente peeked in.

"Is Lenny okay? I was in the schoolroom with the kids. I just heard."

"Take Ginny back with you," Hamid said. "Lenny got hurt and Sergin wants to check him out."

Between them they persuaded Ginny to leave. Hamid was amused that throughout it all, Sergin basically ignored them.

Later when Hamid, Derrick, Lente and Ginny were allowed to visit they found Lenny resting comfortably, his eyes closed.

"It is best he sleep here for the night," Sergin said.

"Did he wake up?" Ginny asked. She was still teary.

At the sound of her voice Lenny opened his eyes. "Ginny?"

"Oh Lenny!" Ginny hurriedly knelt beside the cot. "Are you okay?"

Lenny blinked then gave a weak grin. "Fine," he muttered, before closing his eyes again.

"He has much pain," Sergin explained. "He needs very much to rest."

Ginny squeezed Lenny's hands and bent over to kiss his cheek. "I'll be back tomorrow," she said.

Once again Lenny briefly opened his eyes to give a half smile. Ginny sighed and stood up, unashamedly wiping tears from her eyes.

Angela gave her a hug. "He will be okay. Sergin said the leg isn't even infected so it should heal in no time."

Ginny nodded and sniffed.

"Do you need my help later Sergin?" Angela asked.

"No.... No.... It is best you go to bed. Lenny will be fine. He will be much better in the morning."

As Angela followed Ginny and Lente to the girls' cabin Hamid grabbed her hand.

Lente gave him a curious look. "Are you coming?" she asked Angela.

"She'll meet you later," Hamid replied.

Derrick gave him a wink. "Later," he called as he walked off.

As soon as they were alone, Hamid turned to Angela. "Are you sure he'll be okay?"

She nodded. "It looks bad, but Sergin says he should heal okay."

Hamid sighed.

"I didn't hear the story. What happened?"

Their walk slowed to a crawl as Hamid began explaining. "It was my fault," he finished. "We should never have stopped for the horses."

"We need horses, Hamid. And Lenny will be okay, so stop blaming yourself."

Hamid rubbed the back of his neck. "I just hope so."

"He will be." Angela sounded positive. She paused before adding. "In all the excitement I forgot I have a surprise for you."

"A surprise?"

"Come."

"Where?"

"To your cabin." She refused to say another word until they reached. "You stay here," she instructed. "I'll be right back."

Mystified, Hamid stood by his door and waited. "Do you know what the surprise is?" he asked as Derrick came out to watch.

"No idea."

They didn't have long to wait. Angela soon returned

with a covered basket. She ushered Hamid inside the cabin and Derrick followed uninvited. Angela put the basket on the floor and removed the cover. Inside was a tiny puppy. It could not have been much over one month old.

"Its mother died so you will have to feed it." Angela said as she scooped the puppy into her arms.

Hamid stared at the puppy in horror. He even backed away slightly. He knew what they were doing. They were trying to replace Club. He did not *want* to replace Club. "I don't want it," he said flatly.

Angela stared at him. "I thought you would be pleased," she said hesitantly.

"Well, I'm not. I don't want another dog. Where did you find this?"

"Some of the men went hunting and heard them crying. There were six of them. They were all alone and more than likely the mother is dead because they didn't see any sign of her."

"What did they do with the other puppies?"

"Some of the other villagers took them. I took this one."

The villagers had never kept dogs as pets before, but after seeing Hamid with Club everyone now wanted a dog.

"Well, I don't want it."

Angela looked helplessly at Derrick, but he just shrugged his shoulders. "What should I do with it?"

"I don't know, and I don't care. Just don't leave it here. Give it to one of the other villagers."

"But Hamid..." Angela looked ready to cry.

"Look Angela, I'm tired. Just take the puppy and go." He turned away.

"Hamid...." Derrick tried.

"You too. Just get out. Both of you. I want to sleep."

They both left. Hamid did not turn to watch them leave. Derrick – he was sure it was Derrick – slammed the door with enough force to rattle the roof. Irritated, Hamid turned.... They had left the basket... with the puppy. What he really felt like doing was tossing puppy, basket and all, through the door. He even approached it with that intention. However, the puppy began whining as he lifted the cover of the basket. It was likely hungry. Hamid did not want to care, but he could not toss the puppy out. He recovered the basket, then took the puppy and basket out the door and deposited them both outside Derrick's room.

Not long into his preparations for bed he thought he heard the puppy crying. He frowned. Had Derrick left the puppy outside? Not my problem, he thought deliberately ignoring the puppy's cries. He got into bed and pulled up the covers. The cries seemed even louder. Why me! Hamid grabbed his pillow and covered his ears. It was no good. Furious, he got out of bed intending to order Derrick to take the puppy somewhere else. Flinging his door open he almost tripped over the basket. Hell! Derrick had put the basket right outside his door!

He stared at the basket. Well, this puppy could starve for all he cared. After all – he told them not to leave it here. Hamid looked around. There was no one in sight. Scowling, he again looked down at the basket. The puppy was really creating a racket now, whining and scratching at the basket's cover. His chest felt tight – literally as if someone was squeezing it. Slowly, reluctantly, he bent and took up the basket. Hamid lifted the cover and looked intently at the mongrel. He had not noticed its color before, now he saw that it was black and white – just like Club. How could Angela do that to him? He didn't even realize he was crying until a tear splashed on his arm. He rubbed furiously at his face and sniffed. Without thought he backed into his room with both the puppy and the basket....

Angela had left a crude bottle, made from the stomach of some animal. Hamid carefully took out the puppy and began feeding it. The puppy drank hungrily, then licked Hamid's hand in gratitude. Finally, it fell asleep curled up in his arms. Hamid stared at the puppy. Club had been about six months old when he first got him. This puppy was much smaller. He took a deep breath, trying to relieve the tightness in his chest. He really didn't have the heart to wake it. He went to bed... with the puppy.

Chapter 11

Three weeks later the puppy still didn't have a name. Hamid refused to name it. In fact, he insisted that he wanted to give it away. He and Angela had a rip-roaring argument the day after she gave him the puppy. The entire village must have heard them. Even so, she still refused to take back the puppy and the villagers sided with her. No one wanted the puppy. So, he was stuck with a puppy he swore he didn't want.

Besides Hamid's problem – feeding and caring for his new, unwanted puppy – village life was uneventful. Lenny was fully recovered – well almost. The burns on his leg were more or less healed, but Ginny refused to leave his side. So, when Hamid and Fasraben started making plans to leave the village – it was almost time to pick up more Abnorm children – Lenny was the first to volunteer. Hamid got the distinct impression that Lenny wanted a break from Ginny's fussing.

"How is your leg?" He asked.

"Well enough," Lenny gave him a glare. "And don't say I can't come. It's healed."

Hamid hesitated. He then grinned as he looked up, "Here comes Ginny."

Ginny gave them both suspicious looks. "You're planning something," she stated. "Come on. Out with it."

Hamid could not hide his amusement as he explained.

Ginny was horrified. "No! Lenny, are you crazy? Your

leg is just barely healed."

"Well, I'm going!" Lenny said stubbornly.

"Hamid!" Ginny pleaded. "You have to stop him."

"Well..." Hamid tried to find the right words. He fully understood Lenny's need to get away.

"He can't stop me," Lenny declared. "I'm going no matter what he says."

Ginny looked around for reinforcements and spotted Angela leaving Sergin's cabin.

"Angela!" she called. "Come here!"

Hamid watched as Angela hesitated. Since their big quarrel they had barely spoken to each other. It was stupid – he knew. But... he was still mad because she refused to take back the puppy. He was also mad because just about everyone had taken Angela's side. When they weren't trying to get him and Angela together, they were telling him how dumb or stupid he was acting. They were right – he knew – and that fact only served to worsen his bad mood. Hamid wouldn't be surprised if this were another make up attempt by Ginny.

"Look..." He turned to leave.

"Oh no, you don't," Ginny grabbed his arm.

Hamid shifted uneasily from one leg to another. Angela slowly approached.

"Lenny wants to go on some stupid trip and Hamid is actually going to allow him to," Ginny complained as soon as Angela was close enough.

Angela gave Hamid a brief glance before focusing on Ginny. "Ginny..." she paused and then continued with a little laugh. "I think Lenny needs a break."

"A break!" Ginny was scandalized. "Whose side are you on anyway?"

"There!" Lenny said with considerable satisfaction. "I

knew Angela was a sensible girl." He gave Hamid a side look. "If only some fool I know would recognize and appreciate her."

"Some people are just hard-headed." Ginny released Hamid's arm. "Don't worry Hamid, you aren't the only one." She turned to Lenny and took his arm. "Come along. If you are going on this trip, you need to rest your legs."

Lenny gave Hamid a beseeching look.

"No way. You're on your own." Hamid gave an abrupt laugh. "Traitor!" he added without heat.

Angela stood with him and watched as Ginny led Lenny away. The silence between them was getting uncomfortable, but he didn't know how to break it. Why didn't *Angela* say something? She was hugging herself the way she always did when she was nervous. Now he really felt ashamed. After all she was only trying to help him. And look how he treated her. Hamid kicked at the dirt and stared intently at his shoes.

"Look Angela," he finally muttered. "I guess I'm sorry. I shouldn't have.... I guess I was sort of rude.... You know... the puppy." He lapsed into silence and kicked at the ground again.

"Does this mean we're friends again?" Angela asked. Amazingly her voice held laughter.

Hamid looked up. Angela held a hand over her mouth. She was trying hard not to laugh!

"Okay. Okay." Hamid gave her a reluctant grin. "So I was dumb."

He looked around. Everyone, or it seemed like everyone, was watching them. He grabbed Angela's arm. "Let's go somewhere else."

Angela took a quick look at the open curiosity on the faces of the villagers, and then turned away, her face reddening. "Somewhere private," she muttered.

They settled on Hamid's cabin. He carefully scooped up the puppy, who was playing with a small tree branch. "What should we call him?"

"You want *me* to name him?" Angela stared at him. "Are you sure?"

"Positive."

She gave him an uncertain look. "I don't know. My mind is blank."

"Try," he urged.

After a pause she asked, "How did Club get his name? Oh..." Angela clamped a hand over her mouth. "Oh Hamid, I'm sorry. I didn't mean to remind you...."

"It's okay." Hamid sighed. "I still miss him. But it's okay." He sighed again. "I was eating a club sandwich when Mom finally said I could have a dog." He shrugged. "So he became Club."

They were both silent for a minute. Angela settled down on one of Derrick's creations – a low chair. "How about Basket? He came to you in a basket. Or do you want a name in memory of Club, who was your shadow."

"No. Nothing in memory of... I don't want to replace Club. Basket?" Hamid squeezed down beside her and tried out the name a few times. "Okay. Basket he is."

Angela was still uncertain. "You don't have to use that name if you don't like it. I mean.... I'm not going to act hurt or anything."

Hamid gave her a rueful look. "I know," he said quietly. "I shouldn't have said what I did to you...." He paused, "Why black and white?"

"They were all black and white." Angela was still hesitant. "I didn't really think about it until you mentioned Club's color."

Hamid grimaced. "Don't remind me. I said some awful things to you...."

Angela reached out to touch him. "I know how hurt you were...I know...It's ok."

He stroked the puppy tenderly and wished he could work up the nerve to do the same to Angela. "That's no excuse. I promise I'll never speak to you that way again." His voice was low.

Angela ducked her head and nodded. Gathering his courage, he gently placed the puppy on the ground and hugged her. "I like the name Basket and don't worry; Basket will be himself. Want to hold him?"

They went down on the floor and played with Basket for a few minutes, and then Angela turned to another topic. "Do you think we'll ever get back?"

Hamid rolled over onto his back and watched as she tickled Basket's belly. The puppy loved it! "I don't know." He did not want to totally squash her hopes although he seriously did not believe they would ever return to their own time. "Maybe after this trip we could try the cave one last time.... I don't know."

"What if we don't?" Angela's voice was barely above a whisper.

He looked up then got up and scooted down beside her. "Angela..." Seeing that she was about to start crying he pulled her gently to her feet. They hugged in silence. Of all of them, Angela was the only one still hoping and praying for a return. She seriously missed her parents. Even Lente had matured and moved on.

After a few sniffles Angela pulled away slightly. "I think Ginny and Lenny want to get married."

Hamid nodded. Lenny had told him. The idea did seem final. He hated defeat and somehow to him getting married was almost like publicly admitting that they would never get back. However, he was realistic enough to recognize when to give up.

"Will you let them?"

"Let them?" Hamid stared down at her. "Angela, I can't control Lenny. There is no way I could stop him from marrying Ginny if he wants to."

"You know Lenny listens to you," Angela objected. "And Ginny told me you told him to wait for a while."

"For a while. Not forever."

"Does that mean you think there's a chance that we can get back?"

"Angela…" he didn't know what to say, "Maybe…"

"We'll have to try the caves soon. Before winter comes," she muttered in his chest.

Hamid didn't bother pushing the topic although he was worried about Angela's refusal to let go of the past. However, he was in too good a mood to argue. They lapsed into silence again – a comfortable silence. He gave a deep sigh and hugged her tightly. Their relationship was back on track.

*****

The next few days were busy as they prepared for the trip, yet Hamid was determined to keep his relationship with Angela on track. He wanted to meet with her regularly. Angela, however, seemed to be deliberately trying to avoid him. He became so worried that he finally spoke to Ginny about his concerns. Ginny blamed him.

As she had bluntly stated, "I have Lenny, Lente has Derrick, but you keep blowing hot and cold with Angela."

He did not want to agree. He did not even want to admit she was right about Lente and Derrick although he was aware that they were getting closer. Why didn't he take his relationship with Angela further? Most of the time he wanted to settle down. Yet although he had serious doubts that they would return, he was afraid that making permanent plans would upset Angela even further. Hamid's gut feeling was to wait. Maybe they should set a time limit. There would still be a dilemma. How do you determine how long was long enough? He had a feeling that Lenny would not wait much longer. Ginny clearly was not interested in any delay. They wanted to get married. And sooner or later there would be kids. What then? Would their kids be able to travel back with them? The whole idea was very confusing.

Since he was so ambivalent about their relationship he decided to wait until they returned before forcing the issue with Angela. This time around they planned on taking more food, given that they now had horses for transportation. Plus, they would spend less time hunting.

There were eight volunteers in all; Hamid, Fasraben, Lenny, Derrick, Dystaran, Gamnic and two other Abnorms, Tocentum and Parcher. Hamid was glad that Yorlink had not asked to come with them. He had no reason to distrust the Truman. Yorlink was proving to be extremely good with the training and care of the horses. Still, he just wanted to be one hundred percent sure that they had no traitor in their midst.

On this trip, Lenny was going minus Ginny. Hamid, however, took Basket. He had fashioned a small pouch. It had straps which he fastened around his neck so that the puppy nestled comfortably on his chest. They rode the horses and headed first to the tunnel – it took just under four days – where they picked up about a dozen rifle-looking guns plus enough ammunition to sustain a war.

The supplies were all left by Dystaran's brother.

The Village needed cows. Treber was hoping something could be arranged now that they had the convenience of the tunnel and he had asked Dystaran to leave a message about this need. Next stop was getting the children from the prearranged meeting stop.

So, there they were, traveling in a single file. They were sticking to the old roads, going east, when Fasraben suddenly motioned for silence.

"Listen," he said. "The sounds of horses."

There was dead silence as they listened.

Then Dystaran nodded. "They must be behind us. Quick! We must hide."

It seemed to take forever for them to scramble into the thicker sections of the woods, dragging their horses. It was not yet fall, but the leaves were beginning to change. They would have to be careful because in some areas the woods were no longer a dense thick jungle with unlimited hiding positions.

"Cover the mouth of your horses," Fasraben warned as they waited and watched. It was not long before six horsemen came by. The men looked old, about in their sixties. They too were traveling the old roads in a single file. Each carried a rifle. Within minutes they disappeared down a slope.

Dystaran slowly stood up, careful to keep his hand over his horse's mouth. The last thing they needed was for the horses to call to each other. "They do no go to our village," he said, as he stared after them. "That is no the way."

"Do you think they know about the pick-up?" Hamid asked.

Fasraben answered. "It should no be possible. Yet it is

no a good sign that they travel in this direction."

"So, what do we now?" Dystaran was clearly worried.

"We have the guns," Tocentum suggested. "We could attack them."

Just the thought of firing a gun at a live person gave Hamid the shivers. The last thing he wanted was to act out a wild action movie. What if he actually killed someone?

"How about we just follow them?" he asked. "We should find out where they're going before we attack."

The Abnorms clearly did not like his plan. They wanted to attack now! For a few minutes there was a furious argument as Hamid tried to convince them otherwise. To his surprise, after a significant period of silent contemplation, Fasraben took his side. That did it. Hamid was barely able to hide his amusement as the Abnorms fell in line. There would be no attack.

They remounted after distributing the guns among themselves. Fasraben, Hamid, Lenny and Dystaran got to keep two each, while the others each got one. The ammunition they divided equally. Next, they had to follow the Trumen at a safe distance. The Trumen were keeping close to the old roads so following them was not difficult; keeping hidden was. After less than a mile, Hamid began wondering how sensible his idea was. There were too many of them. They were making too much noise. Sooner or later the Trumen would hear them.

"Fasraben," he turned to the older boy knowing that convincing Fasraben would be the quickest way of achieving his goal, "Maybe we should separate? Some go for the children and one or two of us follow these Trumen."

As usual, Fasraben was silent as he thought about this change of plan.

"We don't know where they are going and the children will be waiting," Hamid added persuasively.

They all stopped and waited for Fasraben to decide. Finally, he nodded. "You are correct." He turned to the Abnorms. "Some will go and collect the children, and some will follow these Trumen."

"I will go with the group collecting the children," Hamid immediately offered.

Lenny and Derrick gave him surprised looks. Hamid understood their shock, but he knew the Abnorms wanted the excitement of following the Trumen. He was more than willing to allow them their excitement. What he wanted was a little peace and quiet. And his gut feeling was that following the Trumen would eventually mean using the guns.

After some discussion, the group split. Lenny, Derrick, Dystaran and Hamid would get the children, while Fasraben and the other Abnorms would follow the Trumen. Fasraben wanted to come with Hamid, but finally decided that as the eldest he could not leave the younger Abnorms on their own. Slowly, Hamid was beginning to realize that the Truman actually liked him, in spite of all that had happened between them. Also, despite Fasraben's irritating lack of emotions he was beginning to respect, perhaps even like Fasraben in turn.

Hamid now looked at Fasraben in silent understanding. Fasraben gave a short nod. "If they come to the same place where the children are I will give you a warning." He turned his horse smartly.

"Try keeping a safe distance away," Hamid cautioned.

Fasraben nodded. "Come," he called to the Abnorms.

"Why?" Derrick asked as soon as they had moved off. He and Lenny had immediately agreed to go with Hamid.

They had kept silent during the group discussion, but Hamid was aware of the questions in their eyes.

He gave Derrick a quick glance. "You didn't have to come with me."

"No, we didn't have to," Lenny agreed, "but we did. So now explain."

"You are confusing Dystaran," Hamid told him with a laugh.

"Just explain."

"No reason. I just wanted..." Hamid shrugged, "I didn't want any more... problems."

"I can't believe you turned down a chance for real some excitement," Derrick said in disgust. "Now we have to go tamely collecting children while the others may enjoy a shoot-out."

"It's not too late to catch up with them," was all Hamid would say.

"I agree with Hamid," Dystaran said. "It is no good to look for trouble."

Derrick gave a snort.

Lenny gave Hamid a considering look and said no more. Hamid was aware that Lenny was now a lot less impulsive since his injury. Well, they had all changed. Never in a million years would he have imagined wishing for a normal school. Yet right now, he wished his biggest decision was figuring out which jeans to wear to class! And look at Derrick – he had actually warned them against stealing the horses. Derrick, who never before turned down a challenge!

As Derrick had predicted, collecting the children was child's play. Even though they were extra careful – the Trumen could be close by – it took just half a day to reach the pick-up point where three Abnorm children were waiting with three Trumen. The Trumen, two men and a woman, were delighted to see them. Two of the children began crying when they realized that their fathers would be leaving them. The other child clutched desperately at the woman. She had dark complexion, yet her features were Asian Indian, with blond hair and very dark eyes.

She held the boy tightly and looked pleading up at Hamid. "Please, my name is Envelo. Will you take me too?"

"Take you?" Hamid repeated stupidly.

"He is my one child," she explained. "And my husband has died."

Hamid looked at Dystaran, who shrugged. "Okay," he decided with a reluctant nod. This would mean that they would have to walk. They didn't have an extra horse for the woman. The two-day return trip would now stretch into three or four days.

As they turned to go, Hamid thought of something. "How will you explain to other Trumen when Envelo and these children just disappear?" he asked the departing Trumen.

The men exchanged grim looks. One answered. "It is normal that children are gone these days. No one will ask. If the child remains in the home the guards will take the child. Parents who wish to save the child will contact the brother of Dystaran. To prevent suspicion many will spread the word that they killed the child. There are many private burials, and it is known that many parents feel it a shame to have the Abnorm child."

"What of Envelo?" Lenny asked quietly.

"We will spread the word that she took her life and the life of her child. It has happened."

"Hell!" Lenny, Derrick and Hamid stared at him in

horror.

As the men walked away the woman gave them a sad smile. "It is as they say. No one will ask. All will suspect the child has been killed – that the child was Abnorm. This is all very shameful. And I am sure it will be suspect that I killed myself. I have told many that I am too sad to live."

Hamid was frowning as he turned his horse. With a Truman patrol here in the Bronx it was clear that the guards suspected something. How much longer before they traced the entire plot to Dystaran's family? The villagers needed to come up with another method of saving the children!

Dystaran interrupted his reflections. "How will we travel back to the village?"

"We can take turns riding," Hamid said. "Whoever is riding can carry a child."

They couldn't get one of the children, the only girl, to sit on the horse – even with Envelo holding her.

"She has a great fear of the horse," Envelo apologized as she tried yet again to get the screaming little girl to stay in front of her.

Hamid lifted the girl down. The child was sobbing hysterically and refused to calm down.

Envelo dismounted. "I will try now to calm her, now I no longer sit on the horse."

Hamid eagerly handed the girl over. Screaming children were definitely not his idea of fun.

"What will...?" Dystaran began. He stopped as a shot rang out.

They froze.

Chapter 12

Hamid jerked his mount so suddenly that the horse nickered and snorted in indignation. "Oh, shoot! What was that?"

"Let's get out of here!" Lenny urged.

"What of the baby?" Envelo asked.

Another shot rang out, quickly followed by a brief volley.

"She will have to scream." Hamid decided. He turned to Dystaran. "Dystaran, you are small. Ride double with Envelo. Lenny and Derrick can each ride with a child. I will take the girl."

"Maybe we should try to help." Derrick hesitated as they were about to start. "What if it is Fasraben?"

"Great!" Lenny muttered. "Just frigging great!"

Hamid gripped the horse's reins as he tried to calm himself. He didn't need this! He didn't need this! Crap!

"Dystaran and I..." he began.

"No!" Lenny objected. "Either we all go check or nobody goes."

This was not the time to argue. "Okay," Hamid gave Envelo a quick look. "Can you keep the children while we check? We will leave you in a safer place."

She didn't want to. Hamid could see she didn't want to, but she really had no choice. He didn't even wait for a reply before leading them away from the clearing.

"We may have to gag that girl for her own good," Derrick said as the little girl's screams continued.

Hamid nodded without stopping. He was not a good rider even under ideal circumstances and was now finding it next to impossible to control his frightened horse as well as an equally frightened child.

"Let's stop here."

Once again they were on one of the old roads. Abandoned buildings lined the road. Quickly, they dismounted and scrambled to find a safe hiding place in one of the buildings. Dystaran helped Envelo. The Truman was now shaking, and unsuccessfully trying to control her tears.

"You should be safe here." Hamid tried to reassure her as he urged her and the frightened children into one of the buildings.

"Promise me. Do no leave me here," she implored.

"We will come back. We promise," Hamid assured her. He just hoped they would be able to keep that promise. What if they got killed? He tried to blank the thought out of his mind as he added to the Truman. "Just try to keep the kids quiet."

"If you have to, gag the girl," Derrick warned again. "Seriously, if she doesn't stop crying soon, gag her. Better that, than having the Trumen find you."

It was drastic, but Derrick was right. "Do as he says. Keep quiet, keep the kids quiet, and just wait here for us."

The boys then turned and started back. Hamid checked his watch. Twenty minutes had passed since the first shot was fired.

"Best we leave the horses," Dystaran advised, as the sound of gunfire got louder.

"Best we get off this trail," Lenny added, once again

mimicking Dystaran's speech pattern.

Good idea, Hamid thought. The last thing they needed was for whoever shooting to back up and find them here. However, he did not relish traveling through the dense woods with horses. He vividly remembered the last time.

"Come! Let's hide the horses and then continue on foot."

They dismounted, each taking a gun and ammunition. Hamid readjusted the puppy, who was now getting agitated. The poor pup. He had endured a screaming child and now this! They moved forward cautiously. At the next bend in the trail, they saw the problem. Fasraben and the others had been ambushed. They were now trapped in the middle of the old road – the horses and trees were their only cover. The Trumen were hiding in the old buildings that lined the road and doing their best to pick them off one by one.

"This is so not cool!" Lenny muttered. "What now?"

Hamid looked around. Six Trumen were possibly hiding in the buildings. As he stood, he finally located five of their positions from the direction of the shots fired. Three were on the left side of the street, two on the right where they were.

"Let's try going that way," he pointed ahead to a road that intersected the one they were presently on.

"You mean to try getting behind them?" Derrick asked.

"Yes."

They crept forward, one by one, making sure to keep trees between themselves and any possible attack. Once on the side road they moved faster, only to stop abruptly. Horses!

"These are the horses of the Trumen," Dystaran said excitedly.

Hamid made a quick decision. "Lenny, you and Derrick stay here and guard the horses." He paused then warned reluctantly, "If any of the Trumen come back, you will have to shoot."

Derrick immediately frowned. "But how will we know who is who? Suppose you have to come back?"

Hamid looked at Lenny.

"Owl hoots?" Lenny suggested.

"Owl hoots?" Derrick said derisively.

"Yes," Hamid decided. "Two owl hoots means it's us. If anyone else comes by, shoot." He looked at Dystaran. "Understand?"

Dystaran nodded, his eyes gleaming with excitement.

Hamid and Dystaran left the other two and began climbing behind the buildings, hoping to surprise one of the Trumen from behind. Hamid handled his gun nervously. He had only ever fired a gun in an amusement park. And, although he had loved high action movies and bloody video games, nothing he had ever done in his life had prepared him to stalk another human. Stalk and shoot. Would he lose his nerve? Would he be able to actually shoot a Truman?

Most of the structures were former apartment buildings. It took only a quick look for Hamid to decide that climbing into them would be dangerous. Not only was there a good chance of breaking a leg or worse, but any movement was also likely to disturb the rubble. The noise alone would alert the Trumen. So, they had to move cautiously, behind and between the buildings. No easy feat, considering the thick woods that blanketed the area. Even the changing foliage worked against them – thinning the forest in some areas and reducing their hiding places.

After negotiating behind yet another building, Hamid motioned Dystaran closer.

"I think someone is in that building," he whispered, pointing to the next building. It was a single-family house. Dilapidated, like all of the buildings. The shots were coming from the second floor and Hamid wondered how the hell the Truman had managed to climb there without falling.

"What do we now?" Dystaran's voice was equally low.

Hamid examined his gun yet again. He did not *want* to kill anyone. And he was not positive he would even be able to shoot anyone at close range. He looked up as another idea occurred to him.

"Let's fire at the Trumen across the street."

"But...."

"We can't creep up behind them without them knowing. But maybe we could confuse the ones on the other side if we fire at them from here."

Dystaran gave a quick nod. They moved closer to the old road then settled down to watch the positions across the street. They didn't have long to wait. In quick succession two shots were fired from two different positions.

"You take the one on your left," Hamid muttered as he crouched.

Hamid missed. Fortunately, Dystaran's shot was true. Pandemonium broke out as the Truman slipped from his perch high between the buildings and fell to the ground. Their friends in the center of the street began cheering. The Truman in the building next to them came running out. Perhaps he thought Hamid and Dystaran were Trumen. Whatever his reason he was coming straight toward them.

"Dystaran!" Hamid yelled.

While not exposed to those on the street, Dystaran was still marveling over his shot and was clearly exposed to the oncoming Truman. He turned quickly at Hamid's shout. Too late! By then the Truman had seen them and had grasped that they were not Trumen. Hamid froze for a second as he realized that the Truman was lifting his rifle to shoot. Dystaran was still exposed! Without thinking, Hamid aimed and fired.

The Truman's chest exploded in a burst of bright red. His entire body jerked before falling back. Hamid's gun clattered to the ground.... He stared at the man in horror. Holy smoke! He was literally shivering, and the puppy began whining in sympathy.

"Hamid! Hamid!" It took a minute before Hamid realized Dystaran was shaking him. With difficulty, he turned to focus on his friend.

Dystaran was looking around nervously. "What do we now?"

A shot ricocheted off the building less than a foot away. Fasraben and the others were now shooting at them!

Hamid swallowed. "Let's move. They know someone is here and they don't know that we're not Trumen."

He started with Dystaran close behind, and then stopped as he remembered his gun. He was so rattled that he had dropped it after shooting the Truman. As he tried to pull himself together, he anxiously patted the puppy, drawing a measure of comfort from the warm wriggly body.

"My gun," he muttered. "I forgot my gun."

"I will get." Dystaran scrambled off.

"Thanks," Hamid murmured.

Dystaran gave him a curious look when he returned.

His eyes were still brimming with excitement, but he seemed to realize that Hamid was having some difficulty coping with the death of the Truman.

"He was the enemy. You saved my life. I thank you."

"That doesn't help," Hamid muttered.

"Soon you will feel better."

Hamid hoped not. Getting better meant getting used to shooting and killing other people. God help them if that became their reality.

"Should I also get the gun of the Truman?"

Hamid shuddered at the thought of picking up the dead man's gun. "I guess so." He took some deep breaths. "I'll be okay. You get the guns then we'll get closer to the other Truman on this side."

"We do the same thing, yes?"

No way! Hamid thought. He was definitely not shooting anyone else. No way was he going to put himself through that again. "I guess so," he muttered again.

The plan was to repeat their success, but it didn't quite work that way. For one thing, Fasraben and the others in the middle of the road seemed to realize that there was some confusion in the ranks of Trumen. They began aggressively locating each shooter after they fired and were also firing at any moving target. That made it doubly dangerous for Hamid and Dystaran to shoot. The last thing they needed was to be mistaken for a Truman. They both tried, or Dystaran did; Hamid made a half-hearted attempt. Neither of their shots found its target and shooting had revealed their positions. After two near misses, and with the bullets ricocheting too close for comfort, Hamid was happy to call it quits. The remaining Trumen obviously had the same idea. There were no more shots from the other side.

"The Trumen are pulling back," Hamid warned. "Shh.... Shh.... Keep down!"

In silence they waited. Sure enough, a Truman quietly crept out of the next building. Dystaran raised his gun.

"No!" Hamid reached forward and pulled down the nozzle. Before Dystaran could comment, he said, "Wait! Let's try to get at least one alive."

The Truman would have to pass right beside them. With luck they should be able to jump him. Hamid quickly whispered his plan. Dystaran nodded he understood. As the Truman got closer, Hamid removed the pouch from around his neck and tied the mouth. The puppy should be safe here for a while, he figured, as he placed the pouch on the ground.

The plan worked beautifully. They tackled the Truman just as he passed, with Hamid landing on his back. Although there was a brief struggle, the Truman really didn't stand a chance of winning – not with two against one. He was soon cursing and screaming, but totally unable to move.

Panting, Hamid looked around cautiously. They had made a hell of a lot of noise. He started getting up just as someone rounded a corner of the building.

"Dystaran," he yelled. "Your gun! Where's your gun?"

Chapter 13

"Do no shoot," someone shouted. "It is I."

Gamnic appeared, crouching low to avoid being shot by anyone from the other side.

"Gamnic!" Dystaran did not hide his relief. They would have been in serious trouble if a Truman had appeared. "We caught one."

"Where are Fasraben and the others?" Hamid asked.

Gamnic stood up.

"Get down," Hamid shouted. "We don't know for sure that they are gone."

Thinking that they were distracted, the Truman tried to break free. Dystaran stopped him simply by using a loose piece of wood to knock the man on the head. He collapsed motionless.

"What happened to Fasraben?" Hamid asked again.

"All are wounded. I alone was not."

Hamid did not get a chance to react. There was a sudden fury of shots.

The horses! The Trumen must have tried to reach their horses. Crap! There was no way he could reach Lenny and Derrick in time to provide help. As suddenly as the shooting began it stopped.

"Come. Let's move from here," he warned. "They may come back to rescue their friends."

"Do we check on Fasraben?" Dystaran asked. "Or go

us to help Lenny and Derrick?"

Hamid eyed him. "We need to help Lenny and Derrick." He turned to Gamnic. "Go tell Fasraben we are here and wait there with them. We're going to help Lenny and Derrick. Just be careful. Remember the Trumen may be coming back this way."

Gamnic turned to the Truman. "What of this one?"

Hamid gave the Truman a brief glance. "Let's gag, tie him up and leave him here." Quickly, they did just that. Dystaran had hit the man pretty hard on the head, but still, he just hoped the man didn't regain conscious while they were away. "Come," he said to Dystaran.

Hamid quickly collected his puppy. There was absolute silence as they approached the area where they had left the horses. Hamid gave two owl hoots. Relief flooded him as he got two in return. Still, they were cautious, and slowly inched their way towards the horses. Nothing happened. No shots. Nothing. The Trumen had left.

Lenny and Derrick rushed out.

"I think I got one," Derrick said with obvious relish.

"If you did there should be only three left." Hamid commented.

"I definitely did."

Lenny nodded. "I think he did. They didn't even hide. They just walked right up to the horses. I think he nailed one. They dragged him away and tried to fire back at us, but I guess they gave up."

"Okay," Hamid said after giving Derrick a curious look. He just didn't get it. Derrick didn't even seem upset! "Let's get the horses and go back to Fasraben and the others."

They collected the Truman that Dystaran had knocked

out and tired him securely to one of the horses. Next they had to help Fasraben.

Fasraben was wounded in the shoulder, conscious, but in a lot of pain. After a quick check, Hamid was hopeful that he would survive. Parcher's wound did not look good. It was lower on his chest – the right side. When Hamid touched the wound, he moaned, but did not regain consciousness. Tocentum was seriously injured as well. Like Parcher, he too was unconscious. On closer examination, Hamid realized that the bullet had only grazed his head. Maybe, just maybe, he too would be okay. One of the horses was wounded so they had to kill it. The other horses were fine. Well at least they now had enough horses. In addition to their horses, they had the six horses left by the Trumen.

After bandaging up the three as best they could, Hamid turned to the Truman. The man was now conscious and watching them with fear in his eyes.

"What do we with him?" Gamnic asked.

Hamid made a quick decision. "I say we release him with a message to his people."

He removed his backpack and took out pen and paper. Quickly he wrote:

'We wish to live in peace and trade with you. We do not wish to fight. If we have to, we will defend ourselves and if you attack us, you will be killed. We have guns, we have horses. We also have other weapons. However, to show you that we really want peace, this man will be allowed to go away unharmed.'

Hamid showed the letter to the others. They nodded. The Truman was given the note and released, minus his horse and gun.

He seemed stunned that he was actually allowed to go free. For a minute he just stood and stared at them. Finally, he gave a short nod. "Thank you for my life." He read the note. "I will try to convince them." Then he was gone.

Hamid knew better than to bet his life on that note saving them from future conflict. Anyway, now was not the time to think about that. Now, he had to get everyone safely back to the village. The two wounded Abnorms were tied to horses. Fasraben insisted on riding himself. They returned to collect an anxious Envelo and the children, and then started on the journey back to the village.

It was a much slower return trip. They were moving along the old roads, so the actual travel was not difficult. The leaves were beginning to change and the sun shining through the branches created an incredible rainbow of hues. Even the air felt different – sharper. Summer was definitely on its way out. In fact, it would have been remarkably scenic, and relaxing were it not for their injured friends. However, with three injured men, the children, plus leading the extra horses of the Trumen – it was not a fun trip.

On the second day the little girl finally stopped screaming. After trying everything including tightly hugging all the children, Envelo had followed Derrick's suggestion and tied the little girl's mouth while they were hiding in the building. Hamid hoped she would not be traumatized for life! Despite his concern, more than once during that first day Hamid was tempted to do the same. He was sure the others had similar thoughts. By the second day Hamid began to have serious doubts as to whether Fasraben and the other injured Abnorms would make it. Shortly after noon Fasraben began slipping off his horse. He was semi-conscious, and they were afraid he would fall, but still he feebly resisted all efforts to get him down. Finally, Dystaran got an idea. They allowed him to sit on the horse but tied him in place. He was bent over, but as least he was still in the saddle.

As it got darker Hamid turned to Lenny. "It's a full moon. Maybe we can continue for a bit longer."

Lenny hesitated. "We're all exhausted."

Dystaran was now leading Fasraben's horse. Lenny and Gamnic each led the other injured Abnorms.

"Best we stop," Dystaran said. "The children."

Envelo agreed. "The children must have a rest. It is no possible that they travel so long."

Hamid reluctantly agreed. He wanted to be back at the village. Now!

They lowered the injured men to the ground. Envelo took care of Fasraben before turning to the other two. Hamid watched her.

"How are they?" he asked.

"Parcher is no good. Tocentum maybe. It is hard to say with a wound to the head."

"Fasraben?"

She shook her head worriedly, "I do no know. It is hard to say. There was much blood loss."

Lenny came up, "We didn't check to see if the bullet was still in them."

"I did," Hamid said. "It's still in Parcher. Fasraben has a hole in his back so I think that means the bullet passed straight through. And the bullet just grazed Tocentum's head."

"So why is he still unconscious?" Derrick had joined them.

Hamid just shook his head. "Don't ask me," he muttered. "I don't know much about medicine."

They were able to get some liquids into Fasraben, but not the other two. Even with the liquids, by the next morning Fasraben was burning with a fever.

"What do we now?" Gamnic asked.

"We are going to make it to the village today, or tonight," Hamid determined. They all silently agreed.

By noon Parcher was dead.

"Are you sure?" Hamid asked. They had all dismounted for another short bathroom and snack break. Gamnic and Derrick were retying Parcher to the horse when they made the discovery.

"Positive," Derrick said.

"I thought he was when we first stopped," Lenny admitted. He and Dystaran had taken down the injured men.

Hamid came over to check. It wasn't that he doubted them. It was just... the disbelief that this was actually happening. He pushed his hands warily through his hair. He needed a haircut, he thought distractedly. How was he going to get his hair cut?

"What do we now?" Dystaran interrupted his disjointed thoughts.

"Just continue." Hamid looked up and around. "We can't leave him here. We still have to take his... his... We still have to take him back. How is Fasraben?" He was almost afraid to ask.

Envelo had taken over the care of Fasraben. "He still lives," was her only reply.

By late evening, the girl had started crying again and soon the other children decided to join in sympathy. Hamid knew they were all tired, but he did not want to stop. A few minutes later the puppy joined the crying chorus. Crap! Hamid exchanged a wild glance with Lenny.

"Should we stop?"

"No." For once Lenny did not have a joking reply. He was pale, his face tight with tension.

Looking around, Hamid saw exhaustion, fear and near panic on the faces of the others. He took a deep breath. "We have to keep going. Ignore the crying as best you can."

The command was impossible, but no one said anything. Like him, they did not want to spend the night sleeping with a dead man. And they did not want to leave his body.

*****

At close to midnight, they finally came within sight of the Bronx River Parkway. Hamid could not hide his relief. They were getting to the village tonight!

"The Village is just over that highway," he pointed.

"Highway?" Envelo asked.

"We just call these wide areas highways." Lenny explained.

"C'mon," Hamid urged. They began riding parallel to the highway, looking for the regular crossing path.

After a while Hamid turned to Dystaran and Derrick. "Dystaran. Derrick. Do you think you could ride to the Village and warn them? Also prepare Sergin. Let him know what happened."

Although they were literally falling down in exhaustion, neither Derrick nor Dystaran objected. They were off within minutes, riding the horses they had been leading, to give theirs a break. It was another two hours before Hamid and the others finally reached the village.

The villagers were somber. Everyone was awake and had heard the news. After helping to carry the injured

Fasraben and Tocentum to Sergin's hut, Hamid went with Treber to Parcher's cabin. Parcher was married and had two young children. Garoci, Treber's wife, was comforting Parcher's wife in their cabin.

"I'm sorry... I'm sorry," was all Hamid could say as he watched helplessly.

"Do no take the blame," Treber sighed. "You did all that was possible."

Hamid did not stay long. There was nothing he could do.... He left Treber and went back to his own cabin. For a long time, he stood, staring silently at the floor, then with a heavy sigh began preparations for bed.

Fasraben and Tocentum were no better the next day. Most of the day was spent preparing for Parcher's burial. Later that evening the entire village turned out for his funeral. By nightfall Fasraben was delirious with fever while Tocentum was still unconscious.

Hamid caught up with Angela as she left Sergin's cabin.

"How are they?" He asked. Last evening he wasn't able to see her because she was busy helping Sergin.

"I think Fasraben will be okay... Tocentum, I'm not sure."

Hamid breathed a sigh of relief. "You're sure about Fasraben?"

Angela nodded. "His wound is only slightly infected. He should be okay. And Sergin says the fever may break today."

As they stood chatting, Lente, Derrick, Ginny and Lenny joined them.

"What's up?" Hamid asked noting their serious expressions.

"Let's go to your cabin," Lenny suggested.

Hamid looked at Angela, but she was as mystified as he. She shrugged. "I've been with Sergin all day," she said by way of explanation.

Lenny and the others refused to say another word until they were inside Hamid's cabin. Then Lenny became the spokesman.

"Ginny and me, we're going to get married. We'll wait a few days then announce it to everyone."

Hamid looked at Ginny. She grinned in excitement. "We thought about it like you said, Hamid, but we want this, even if we get back."

"Which I doubt will happen," Lenny inserted.

"We should wait," Hamid insisted stubbornly. "We should wait before doing anything permanent."

"Wait!" Lenny was shaking his head. "For how long? We could wait forever, waiting. After this trip and all that's happened... I don't want to wait."

Hamid could understand that. Death could come at any time. His mind shied away from thoughts of the Truman he had shot. Last night he had relived the shooting in an all too realistic dream. Still... to accept... to move on with their lives... He wanted to convince Angela first. "Okay. What about going back to the cave one more time?"

Derrick gave a snort. "Seriously Hamid, do you really believe that cave will ever get us back?"

He did not – not really. He frowned as he began pacing the cabin. "Maybe not, but shouldn't we at least try one more time?"

"Maybe we could," Angela added. "Just for peace of mind."

"Fine with me," Lenny shrugged. "But Ginny and me, we still want to get married – before we leave."

Before Hamid could comment, Derrick said in a rush, "Lente and I want to get married too."

"What!" Hamid stared at him. "Are you crazy?"

Derrick backed away from the fury in Hamid's eyes. "I don't mean right now," he said defensively.

Hamid took a step forward. "You'd better mean not ever!"

"Now look here..."

"Lente is not marrying you and that's that." Hamid's hands were clenched by his sides.

"You're not my father," Lente burst out. "You can't stop me from getting married."

"I don't believe I'm hearing this. Lente you're thirteen! Thirteen! Are you crazy? Mom and Dad would have a fit!"

"Well, they aren't here," Lente said defiantly.

"She's right." Derrick was deadly serious. "Get real, Hamid. Look around you. Even twelve-year-old are married. Besides, I told you I didn't mean right now. I mean in a maybe a year's time. I was only letting you know our plans. And I'm not letting you mess up our lives just 'cause you can't accept facts."

"I mean it Hamid," Derrick said, as Hamid remained silent.

"You are the only one still refusing to make permanent plans for our lives here," Lenny pointed out with a meaningful look at Angela.

For a minute Hamid stared at them all, then he turned away and restlessly began pacing again. The others just waited.

They were right about dine permanency of their lives here. If he was honest with himself he would admit his worry was for Angela. She had not yet accepted that they would be here forever and he was trying to please her by offering her false hope. There was also Ginny's theory that Angela felt rootless because he refused to commit to a serious relationship. It was a vicious circle, and it was time to bring it to a halt.

Lente spoke up. "I still miss Mom and Dad. But if we have to live here, or even if we get back, I want to marry Derrick."

Hamid didn't answer her, although he had to admit that Derrick had grown up a lot in the past few months and since she started teaching the younger kids Lente had definitely matured. Maybe… Right now, he still could not see himself agreeing to their getting married anytime soon. Perhaps in a year… He would have to talk with Lente later – alone. "So do we try the cave again or not?"

"Try it when?" Ginny asked. "Summer is over. You know how quickly the weather can change. I don't want to get caught away from the village in a snowfall."

Ginny was right. Hamid finally gave up. He could see the determination on both Lenny's and Ginny's faces – they wanted to get married. Besides, he really didn't believe that the cave would get them back. It was just… a reluctance to give up totally on the past by making drastic changes. And marriage was as drastic a change as you should get. But it was time to move on. What he needed to do was get the others out of here and have a good, long chat with Angela. He really liked her, and he knew she liked him.

"Okay."

"Okay, what?" Lenny scowled at him.

Ginny, Lente and Derrick just looked puzzled while Angela was frowning, worrying, as was usual. He ignored the others; gave her a smile and was reassured when she smiled back.

"Okay, no trip. We start planning your wedding." Hamid nodded to Lenny and Ginny before turning to Derrick. "You and Lente are on hold and I want to talk to Angela so you can all get out."

Lenny didn't need to be told twice. He dragged a giggling Ginny out and Lente had a huge grin on her face as she followed Derrick.

As soon as the door closed behind them, Hamid pulled Angela close. No more waffling. Angela was his girlfriend, and it was past time that he reassured her on that fact. Maybe they would find another way back, but it didn't matter. And really, it was getting harder to imagine their return. In the meantime, they had to live. And right now, this village was their life. They had lucked out. It really was amazing that, despite being intruders in this world, these people had totally accepted them.

Preview –The Intruders, The Battle For The Bronx

Chapter 1

Hamid watched nervously as Treber, the tribe's leader, handled his maps. The site of their village was not safe. It was on the flat lands of the former Bronx Botanical Gardens. There were just too many access points which made defending the village a nightmare. They had survived one major skirmish with the Manhattan tribe, the Trumen, but they were the smaller group with fewer resources, they needed to take defensive actions soon, hopefully before the Trumen's next major offensive move. It had taken Hamid a year to convince Treber that they had to move. Treber and just about every Abnorm … oops forgot … they had decided to drop the negative Abnorm title given to them by the Trumen…. They were now the Mosholus. All the Mosholus had relatives and friends in Manhattan. They were reluctant to move. *He* was reluctant to move. The problem was they could be wiped out in another battle. After working hard to convince Treber to move the entire village he could not now refuse Treber's request to see his maps.

Good thing his friends Derrick and Lenny were not here to see him sweating. They both laughed at his obsessive-compulsive habits. Hamid tried distracting himself by thinking on what they had accomplished so far. A year ago they were six carefree teens enjoying summer in the Bronx. Then, in a freak of nature, the six friends had time travelled three centuries into the future – while exploring an abandoned park in the Bronx.

Unfortunately, civilization as they knew it had vanished and they had landed in the middle of what was turning out to be a major conflict between two tribes. Fortunately for them they were rescued by the Mosholus and had settled comfortable into village life where they had all made signification contributions. He and his friends had been instrumental in getting the villagers to agree to the name change because the six had all come to hate the 'Abnorm' title. The village now had a thriving school, thanks to Ginny and Lente, and Lenny and Derrick had worked wonders in building furniture and farm equipment. There was also Angela's considerable contribution to their health care.

"I do no understand," Treber was pointing to the map. "Is this a river?"

It had taken some time for the six friends to understand the Mosholus strange speech pattern. Hamid was about to respond when the door burst open, and Lenny rushed in.

"Angela is hurt!"

"What?" Hamid jumped up scattering papers and his precious maps. "What happened?" Angela was his girlfriend. They had had a rocky start and it had taken him the better part of the past year to stabilize his relationship with her. "How can she be hurt?

"She was with Sergin, picking herbs," Lenny said grimly. Sergin was the village medic. Lenny did not wait for Hamid's reaction. He was already rushing out the door.

Hamid hurried after him and broke into a run as Lenny continued. "We think they were attacked by snipers."

"What about the guards?" Treber asked. In the past year they had devised a rotating guard system. It was not a perfect system. They had decided that the village was indefensible. The problem was deciding where to go—definitely further north but where?

"I don't know. Let's find out what happened. Where are the others?" He called out to Lenny. By others he was not referring to the other villagers but his three other friends.

"Ginny and Lente are at the school. I sent someone to call Derrick. He was at the workshop on the other side of the village."

Hamid nodded. Six months ago, Ginny had married Lenny. Lente was Hamid's younger sister and the youngest of the six. Hamid was still trying to delay her proposed marriage to Derrick. Although now, he was not as violently opposed to them getting married as he was before. At fourteen she was already a year past the marriage age of the average girl in the village. They had to adapt to the culture here and already life with the Mosholus had changed them all. Derrick was no longer an angry, easily frustrated teen. Lenny became thoughtful and cautious after getting seriously burned in an accident. Had he changed? Well, he was more accepting of Derrick and Lente seeing each other but he knew that despite repeated teasing, he was still an obsessive, compulsive perfectionist.

"Where're you going?" Hamid had veered away from Lenny.

"Cabin...gun..." Hamid continued running. Lenny followed.

"I also will get mine… and meet with you." Treber changed direction and began shouting to the other villagers as he ran. "Get your guns, meet with Hamid!"

Minutes later they were gathered around as Tocentum, one of the villagers explained what he saw.

"I went to consult with Sergin. I was on the small rise when I heard the shots."

"You said Angela was hurt." This was Hamid's major concern.

"I saw her fall. I was too far to help. I also saw Sergin fall. I did no see the shooter so I ran back for help."

"What of the guards?" Hamid repeated Treber's earlier question. He could barely contain his impatience to be off but a year among the Mosholus had taught him to be cautious. Within months he and his friends had appreciated the difference between shooting at the enemy in a video game versus a real-life shootout.

Treber began calling our orders. "You and you," he pointed to two Mosholus, "Go with Tocentum and find the guards. Go with care. There may be an ambush." He turned to Hamid but paused as Fasraben and Derrick approached.

"What has happened?" Fasraben was Treber's son. Although he had the same blue eyes and brown complexion of his father, he had the aged look that was typical of all Truman.

"Angela?" Derrick interrupted before anyone could reply.

"We're not sure what happened." Hamid noted that both Fasraben and Derrick had guns. "Let's go. I'll tell you what we know as we move. We need to find Angela." A year ago he and Fasraben were barely speaking to each other, then Fasraben saved Lenny's life. Life and death situations had a way of putting petty quarrels in perspective.

Treber nodded his approval.

The three Mosholus headed towards the higher ridges while Hamid, Lenny, Derrick, Fasraben and Treber plus four others hurried across the flat farmland to the woods at the periphery of the village. They walked in single file and carefully navigated the lightly wooded area. After about half a mile, Treber raised his hand in a signal to stop. They would have to crawl on the ground from this point forward. The land dipped and from their vantage point they could see clear across a wide expanse of the woods. It was summer so the dense undergrowth could be hiding an entire army. However, were exposed. This meant that others would be able to see them. But where were Angela and Sergin?

Treber signaled that they would continue downhill. Hamid touched him. He wanted to travel along the higher ground. He did not want to lose their advantage and become sitting ducks in the depression. He softly explained his plan to Treber. After thinking for a minute, Treber decided that he liked Hamid's plan. The group set off along the higher ground, they took care to keep on the village side of dip in the land to avoid being seen. They did not get far before Treber again signaled for silence. He pointed. In the distance two Trumen were moving away from them travelling towards the deeper woods.

Hamid's heart sank. Trumen! Here! Less than a mile from their village. This meant the Trumen had found them. It had been only six months since their last confrontation with the Trumen. He had hoped for more time. This was going to be a disaster!

Thank you for reading
The Intruders
by Jo Dinage

About the Author

Jo Dinage describes herself as a people watcher and enjoys trying to figure out what motivates others. She is the author of 5 young adult novels.

Author's Note

The rapid aging of individuals as described in this story is truly fiction and does not conform to any known disease. However abnormal aging is a real condition.

One abnormal aging disease is called Hutchinson-Gilford progeria syndrome and was first described in 1886. It is a very rare genetic condition – there are only approximately 130 cases reported worldwide. The condition is characterized by the dramatic, rapid appearance of aging beginning in childhood. The affected children typically look normal at birth and in early infancy, but then grow more slowly than other children and do not gain weight at the expected rate. By the age of eighteen to twenty-four months they are shorter than normal with faces disproportionately large for their heads. They also develop a characteristic facial appearance including prominent eyes, a thin nose with a beaked tip, thin lips, a small chin, protruding ears and prominent scalp veins.

Hutchinson-Gilford progeria syndrome also causes hair loss – the child is usually bald by age four with aged-looking skin, joint stiffness and other aging abnormalities such as loss of fat under the skin leading to thin, taut, dry and wrinkled skin. This condition however does not affect intellectual development or the development of motor skills of the child such as sitting, standing, and walking. In fact, children with the condition usually have above normal intelligence and although their bodies look frail they enjoy childlike activities, limited only by their symptoms of aging.

Children with Hutchinson-Gilford progeria syndrome experience severe hardening of the arteries (arteriosclerosis) beginning in childhood. This can lead to cardiac conditions such as heart attacks or cerebrovascular disease such as strokes at an early age. These serious complications can worsen over time and are often life-threatening. Unfortunately, there is no cure for Hutchinson-Gilford progeria and affected individuals rarely live beyond twenty years with an average life span of only thirteen years.

Another progeroid syndrome is Werner's syndrome. This condition is a little more common and is also known as "adult progeria." Werner syndrome typically does not affect the child until puberty. The affected teenagers do not have a growth spurt and begin to develop characteristic aged appearance including graying, hair loss, hoarse voice and thin and hardened skin. They also develop a "bird-like" facial appearance and have thin arms, legs and trunk due to abnormal fat deposits. As with children with Hutchinson-Gilford progeria syndrome, Werner's syndrome results in a shorter life span, generally due to cardiac or other age-related conditions. The average age span of those who start suffering from the condition as teenagers is forty to fifty years.

To donate or get involved in finding a cure for these rare conditions visit The Progeria Research Foundation – web site: http://www.progeriaresearch.org/ – or the Genetics Home Reference – web site : http://www.ncbi.nlm.nih.gov – both provide consumer friendly information and current research about the effects of genetic variations on human health.